JUSTHIS

A NOVEL

by
CURT RUDE

Cover & interior design by Indie Author Services
Edited by Gary Anderson

ISBN 978-0-9884319-0-4

If you can think it, you can say it.
If you can say it, you can write it.
This excellent advice was offered to me by my loving wife.
Thus, Peggy, this work certainly must be dedicated to you.

—PROLOGUE—

It was a typically dreary Halloween evening, full of warning of a winter soon to arrive in all its wind-driven glory. Driving fast, perhaps too fast in the cold blowing rain, Martin felt things could be made right. A sickening thud and a shattered windshield brought him back from his obsessive thoughts.

"Christ!" he thought. "A deer? Not a kid—god, not a kid or a trick-or-treater."

Life suddenly downshifted from fast forward to slow motion. The screeching of tires seemed to last forever.

Martin leaped from the car, unable to deny the reality of what he was seeing. His eyes pulled him toward the carnage and a gruesome spectacle, the result of being in the wrong place at the wrong time.

A large, bloody mass lay in a twisted, morbid position. Ribs, blown from the chest cavity and pointing toward the cold, uncaring sky while holding the torso up in a macabre fashion, met his gaze. What seemed to be a never-ending pool of gore engulfed the scene. Thick globs of meaty paste were spattered everywhere.

Martin's shock-numbed mind told him to check for vitals, but his police training told him that would be foolish—the reaction of the sort of untrained, stupid civilians who were the butt of cop jokes. No, this spectacle that had once been a woman, a daughter, or maybe a mother, was now a bloody puddle of steaming meat and broken bones. Without even realizing it, he had stepped on a chunk of waxy yellow fat that clung to the sole of his shoe. This pile—a former living, breathing person—was giving up its warmth to the cold, indifferent night. The skull had been split in two from the force of the impact and the eyes pointed in different directions and seemed to be observing, but not comprehending.

Martin thought about the size of the impending lawsuit, but then thought of the meat scattered all over the road. Lawsuits, meat, blood. He even thought of how the blood always reminded him of gutting a deer. Thoughts were screaming through his adrenalin-fueled mind without any real direction or order.

He must have been in shock to be thinking so wildly. Christ, what next? He was brought back to the present by a woman screaming that she had called 911.

"Do you need anything else?" she called out.

"Yeah," he thought, "I need to get away."

It was like that airline commercial he saw while watching games on Sundays. He needed to get a long god damned way from that mess!

Martin couldn't believe fate had put his sorry ass into such a situation. Such things were supposed to happen to other sorry-ass bastards. He wasn't a cop just doing his job and looking for clues at the scene of a 10-54 fatal traffic accident. He'd been the *driver*.

Jesus Christ, it was different being the driver and not just a wise-ass cop on the scene. Oh, for Christ's sake, he had worked thousands of accidents, but never thought it would happen to him.

He found himself thinking, "Let this be some kind of dream."

But it wasn't, and Martin, locked in a staring contest with the woman's dying eyes, suddenly realized that he had looked into those eyes before.

—Chapter 1—

The Beginning
"Star Star" (The Rolling Stones)

Chimlyn heard a pigeon, or perhaps it was a dove, cooing softly. He and his buddies had gotten together to enjoy some underage drinking, but the town cop and some deputies showed up to spoil it. Everybody had scattered, leaving all the beer and other drunken possibilities at the scene of the crime. The cops had somehow found out they had planned to party at the barn, which had put an end to everything. No puking, burping, or playing grab ass. Life could be so unfair. If he had gotten apprehended (cop lingo for *busted*), life would've been even more unfair.

Chimlyn had ditched himself under a pile of straw in the hayloft. He just couldn't get busted. His coach would kick him off the team, and football was too important to him. It was the only reason the other kids hung out with him.

He didn't move a muscle for what seemed like hours, and it worked. He wasn't one of those who got dinged for consumption by a minor. He made a promise on the spot that would last one whole week: no more drinking.

He left his hiding place only when he heard the prolonged sound of silence—no "10-4" or "How many perps did ya cite?" or any other of the language the law used.

When Charles Paul Pullet was born, his parents felt a lot of things, including relief that both mother and child were healthy. They had thought that advancing age and disappearing menstrual cycles had tossed them onto the "grandparent" heap, but their plans of escaping Minnesota winters by heading south were instantly dashed and his father was suddenly standing in line at the store, his cart filled with diapers and baby formula.

"Why, look, Father, he's a perfect baby," his wife had said, and in her world, everything was just as it should be—including her son, who could do no wrong in her eyes.

As Charles struggled with the usual issues of growing up, his mother was always there. She held her precious son close, pleading with him to stay away from hooligans—which included anyone his own age.

"They're nothing but trouble, and Mother won't stand for it," she'd say. "You better stay away from those kids. Not a one of 'em will amount to a hill of beans. You come straight home and practice the piano. Then we'll have our DQ date!"

Any desires that involved hanging out with people his own age weren't just discouraged—they were totally squelched. Mother even loved to hear him, in all his misery, struggle at the piano.

Charles's father had once dared to question his wife (after finding some liquid courage in a six-pack), asking, "Why can't ya just let 'im get dirty like other kids? Yer gonna end up with a momma's boy. Is that what ya want?"

His father had only been allowed to utter that entire sentence because she had never expected such a thing. She stopped drying the dish she was holding, slowly turned to face her withering husband, and said, "Who asked you, you ol' fool? I should never have allowed you to go out. This is the thanks I get. I've been home all day trying to do right by my Charles—and *you* come home drunk! Why do I put up with it? What would Charles think if he knew what kind of father he has?"

"W-what?" his father had managed to stammer before retreating back to the relative safety of his silence once more.

For his part, Charles basked in the radiance of Mother Pullet's approving smile. He knew she loved him dearly and he wanted to please her more than anything.

"Why, look at you. You're Mother's Sweetie Little Gherkins—and I love you dearly," she said to her little boy, who was on his way to his school's Halloween party dressed as a little law enforcement officer.

"Mother, I want to grow up to be a real policeman," Charles announced.

"We shall see, dearest Charles, but remember, you can be anything you want, and you wouldn't want to worry me half to death, would you?"

Charles's concern for his mother's wishes resulted in the loss of many of his boyhood ambitions. His friendless world of nothing but a happy mother and piano practice squeezed him into a tight ball of frustration, and he longed for more.

"Yes, Mother, I'll be home as soon as my studies are in order."

"Oh, Charles, you're such a joy to me."

Charles managed well enough until another urge started demanding attention—the urge. He fertilized it with impure thoughts and dirty picture books. The urge made him lick dirty pictures and fondle his wee-wee friend. He knew other boys who got to hold girls' hands and imagined them holding a whole lot more, but he wouldn't have done it, even if he could have. Mother would have frowned on such behavior—and besides, she watched him like a hawk. Thus Charles's life revolved around dirty pictures in private and piano practice in public.

Martin's mother had met her husband when he was home on leave after completing basic training. She wanted off the farm with enough money to buy bananas whenever she wanted. He simply wanted someone good-looking to do something with his banana whenever he wanted. It was a match made in heaven. Their respective desires resulted in a sweet sixteen-year-old getting pregnant in no time flat. The first baby was soon followed by a second.

Young men in the military are at times prone to mistakes. After an evening of revelry that included drinking and driving, Martin's father was involved in a crash and was laid to rest, not to sleep, but to decompose. His widow then fled with her two children back to Minnesota at about the same time her folks had sold the farm and retired to the quaint community of Red Wing.

Martin developed an appreciation for police officers at an early age. On one particular evening, his mom had been barhopping and returned home with a large male escort, which was nothing unusual. Martin, then a bony, knock-kneed young boy, was sound asleep.

As muffled, beer-slurred insults morphed into screaming and hollering, he woke up. He heard a sound like a table crashing into a wall and chairs being scattered as he lay in bed, his eyes closed tightly and sheer terror gripping his soul. Mom was at it again. She had a knack for bringing out the worst in guys. When she was keeping company with her weekend buddy, Mr. Intoxication, shit just happened.

Martin had to make like he was the world's soundest sleeper and his mom hoisted his terror-stricken body out of bed and awkwardly carried him toward the dreaded encounter. His heart was pounding wildly as she set him down on his feet on the cold linoleum floor of the kitchen. To his horror, he soon found himself standing in a puddle of urine. He hadn't even known he had to go potty.

As Martin stood watching, his mother began hammering her male companion with invectives. Martin couldn't believe she was brave enough—or drunk enough—to risk hurling such horrendous insults at such a giant man, who just stared down at her in silence, clenching and unclenching his fists.

"Show me what a big man you are. What ya gonna do, hit a lady, you fuckin' bum!" his mother shouted.

Showing enormous patience, the man stood his ground, panting like a bull and glaring at her with bulging bloodshot eyes.

"I'm calling the cops so they can haul your drunken ass to the slammer, you stupid son of a bitch!" his mom screeched.

Apparently that comment pushed the huge man over the edge. His face filled with rage, he lumbered forward, snatched a steak knife from the counter and raised it above his head.

Undaunted, Martin's mom taunted, "Look at you, Big man! What are you going to do with that puny knife—and see what you did? You went and made my son piss himself, you asshole!"

The man paused for a moment, then turned and cut the cord on the wall phone before lumbering forward again. Just before he reached Martin and his mom, there was a loud banging at the kitchen door.

"Police! Open up!" a deep male voice shouted from outside.

Before anyone could move, the door flung open and two policemen barged into the kitchen. They cuffed and led the huge man outside. Then one of the officers returned and began asking questions. Martin tried to catch his breath and answer the policeman's question's, but he really didn't know what to say. If he said bad things about the man, he might come back and murder him. If he said bad things about his mom, she might beat him. Choked by his thoughts and emotions, the only thing Martin could do was cry uncontrollably.

For her part, his mom acted as if nothing unusual had happened, concentrating on her embarrassment at having a young son who would pee in the middle of the kitchen floor. "For Christ sake, Martin, you're too old to be pissin' your pants," she said drunkenly. "Don't tell me you were scared. What was he going to do with that tiny knife?"

The police officer ignored Martin's mom's raving and spent a good deal of time trying to comfort the trembling little boy. He even offered to help clean up the mess so that Martin's older sister, Wrenny, wouldn't see it when she got home.

His mom was already in bed, snoring loudly, before Martin and the officer had finished mopping up the mess.

"Hey, are you gonna eat them?" Agnes asked, pointing at Charles's fries.

"Naw, go ahead."

Charles always gave into girls. He loved, talking to girls, any girls, even if it meant giving up some french fries. Charles thought Agnes looked like a baby hippo. She wasn't small by any means, but there were fatter girls in the class. He'd even fuck her if he had the chance. The difference between fucking ugly girls and pretty girls was that the ugly ones would thank you afterward.

Agnes finished off his fries, using the last one to mop up the remaining ketchup on the plate. Charles thought he might not be able to fuck her if he ever had to watch her eat again.

"You still carrying that medal thingamajig around?" she asked while licking her fingers.

Ever since third grade, Charles had carried one of his father's war medals. It had George Washington's face on it and he loved how it looked. It also made him feel like something he wasn't.

"Yeah, what of it?" Charles asked defensively.

"Well, you don't have to go and get all pissy about it. You know the guys have started calling you Badge 'cause of that medal. I just wanted you to know. They saying ya carry it around so you can play pocket pool."

Charles already knew that. He also knew that no matter what they called him, he'd continue to carry father's medal—until he could get one of his own. Changing the subject, he asked, "Michael Jackson or Donny Osmond—who's better?"

Though Charles argued for Michael Jackson, Agnes said derisively, "God, both those guys are old news. You should really get with the times, Badge—I mean, Charles."

Several birthdays went by, but Martin could never come to grips with his mom's actions. She somehow avoided getting her ass kicked on the weekends, but Martin figured she was just incredibly lucky. Outside of pushing and shoving on the weekends, all seemed to be well in her world.

For his own part, Martin didn't completely turn his back on Mr. Intoxication. That guy could deliver a shitload of fun in the form of sloshed sweethearts. If god had created anything better than drinkin' girls, Martin figured, he must have kept it in heaven.

Even so, Martin was fortunate enough to know at an early age what he wanted to do with his life. He was going to stand on the door step of misery and serve up relief—which meant he would eventually get to kick Mr. Intoxication's ass. He could never become a cop if he had a police record, though, so he had to be careful that his drinking and horsing around didn't result in an arrest.

Some of his friends chided him for his ambition, saying things like, "You're way too cool to be a cop. They're just power-hungry dudes who drive around running stop signs just 'cause they can!"

He'd retort, "No way! I won't be like that. I'm gonna bust bad asses."

Martin had stared down his monsters, and he truly wanted to make the world better for other scared shitless little guys—like the kind of little guy he used to be.

When Charles "Badge" Pullet graduated from high school, he exceeded his mother's expectations. He had lived a mushroom-like existence in her shadow.

People looked through him as his Mother informed them about his future plans at the graduation party. "Charles will be holding down his job at the plant. It's a good job, and now that he's more educated, he'll be in a position to move into management."

Mother smiled while Badge remained silent. The Urge was now his friend more than it had ever been. Badge pretended he was going to become a rock-n-roll star so babes would throw themselves at him, but he couldn't sing and his piano lessons had finally come to a merciful end. Yet he still felt he was the next Elton John and wanted to believe that he would one day be discovered and immediately surrounded by a harem of groupies.

Badge clung to the belief that he was too special to waste away in the Old Dutch potato chip factory. He was the owner of an exceptionally large, but pitifully unemployed penis that he desperately wanted to put to work. After graduation, he had a diploma, his intact virginity, and a useless job producing potato chips.

Badge became a regular customer at smut shops in Minneapolis, favoring the ones on Hennepin Avenue. Mother would never approve of his friend, the Urge, and what it made him do. The Urge demanded that he score one of the whores that hung around every intersection.

As Badge drove around in his Buick Skylark, contemplating the unthinkable, the Urge taunted, "Come on Badge, quit this limp dick crap. You know you want it."

He generally managed to beat the Urge back into place, but a few days later he'd find himself again being pulled back toward the center of a whirlpool. The Urge was nothing if not patient and was always there waiting for his return. Off to the bookstores he'd go, barely making it back home in time to relieve the pressure by hand.

Mother finally decided that it was time for her Charles to have a special someone in his life. "The poor boy needs a proper girl to keep company with," she told his father. "What about Matilda's daughter, Agnes. They went to school together. I play bridge with Matilda on Wednesday. I'll see what can be done about it."

Father considered the Agnes proposal a terrible idea, but he wasn't about to voice any objection.

Chimlyn was everyone's friend, but he was careful to never get too chummy, for fear that they'd find out he didn't "get it." The older kids called him a 'tard and a reject because he wasn't a brainiac, so he just laid low to remain invisible and thus be safe from the name calling.

He discovered a cache of old books in a box in the attic while playing hide-and-seek one afternoon. He read and read, asking Ma what various words meant, thinking that if he could just read enough books, he'd get smart.

Abraham Lincoln was a president. Chimlyn could remember that, but he couldn't seem to remember the little things, like the name of Lincoln's wife. Chimlyn knew logging was important and a Minnesota man named George Boorman had cut lots of trees down, but he couldn't remember why.

A number of glass plates were also in the box Chimlyn found in the attic, carefully wrapped in tissue paper. They showed the Minnesota State Capitol while it was being built. Ma called it "constructed."

The magazines he liked best were the *Popular Mechanics*.

"Well, now, why don'tcha bring some of those magazines down so we can put together somma them there ex-pur-ments," Chimlyn's favorite uncle, Lobs, said, spitting out a stream of tobacco juice. "Yesiree! Take this project right here. Ya fill a bucket up with water and then the water gets dumped from one bucket into another, like an hour glass, and finally—bang—it can do something."

Chimlyn spent many afternoons with Lobs. They were the best times of his carefree life, afternoons building projects in Lobs's shop.

As fall approached, so did football season. Chimlyn was a big boy and was going to be a tackle for the Madelia Blackhawks football team.

Lobs rubbed the bristles on his chin and shifted the cud of tobacco in his mouth. "Yeah, I 'spect yer gonna kick some ass. It's be a nice way to spend Saturday afternoons, watching ya stomp lil bastards into the ground."

Badge never managed to become a rock 'n' roll star, but he did manage to amass an enormous pile of smutty video tapes and magazines. He also scored his first blow job, thanks to some of the guys at work. He was at a bachelor party and some guys showed up with working gals. Badge would always remember the name of the girl he was with: Lucia. The moment she popped him into her mouth and started sucking, he lost his heart and soul—and fell in love.

"Baby, if you ever get a cravin' for some sweetness, you just look Luscious Lucia up," she told him when she was done. "Here's the number of the ol' candy store."

She then handed him a card bearing her "personal" phone number—and they hooked up again and again since that time. While Badge diligently screwed Lucia into a higher tax bracket, he hoped he was becoming something special to her—but she just wanted him to be done so she could snag a few more bucks before calling it a night.

Knowing she had hooked a sucker, Lucia filled his head with sob stories. "Hon, I got bills to pay 'cause my kids got some sorta flu or something. Could ya kick in an extra ten spot this time?" Sometimes she resorted to flattery. "Man, oh, man, you got a big unit there, mister! Lord, I'm gonna haveta charge you extra for poking fun at me with that thing! I might get hurt!"

Badge had a hard time saying no, and he honestly wanted to believe that she felt something for him. After all, she often told him that she only charged him to help pay her bills. To Badge, that implied that she'd one day give it to him for free. He was also a sucker for stories about her worthless husband and kids.

"That mothafucker," she'd say. "All he ever does is lay around all day long. He just sits on the damned couch and makes me do the providing."

She accompanied her hard luck stories with a sad expression that could have gotten her an Academy Award nomination—but Badge didn't care. Talk like that caused the Urge to blow, instantly ending the transaction, which both pleased and perplexed Badge. He loved making the Urge so happy, but he often wished it could take longer to do it.

Asking Luscious Lucia to stop talking about her hard luck wasn't an option. He had real feelings for her and wanted to be there when she needed someone to talk to. Lucia, shrewd operator that she was, knew exactly what to say to pull Badge's trigger so she could get back on the street as quickly as possible without losing one of her most loyal customers.

Badge gave up on becoming the next Mick Jagger, but he still hoped to find a way to distinguish himself somehow. He was never without his father's medal, except when he was with his girlfriends. If the Urge was hungry and Lucia was nowhere to be found, Badge hooked up with other girls who occasionally helped themselves to all the money in his wallet after he had dozed off, leaving him high and dry when he woke. It never really bothered him much. The release was worth it, and the loss of money was something he could tolerate.

However, his father's medal was irreplaceable, and he never would have forgiven himself if the medal had somehow slipped from his possession. The day would come when he'd get his own shiny badge, but until then, his father's would have to do.

In his heart, Badge knew that if and when he got hired as a police officer, his life would have to change, beginning with saying good-bye to the ladies of the evening. Although Luscious Lucia seemed to understand him, she would have to be left behind. After all, it was against the law to purchase such pleasure even, if no one was getting hurt.

"Why can't I pay for it?" Badge found himself wondering at times. "It's the same as taking a girl to the movies or dinner. I'd pick up the bill and hope I'd get asked into the bedroom."

There was no doubt about it: some laws sucked big time.

When the Normal police department finally hired Badge, he celebrated with his mother and father by going to Cecil's delicatessen for plates of chicken liver. Badge would have preferred chicken wings, but he always ate what Mother ordered for him. He also had to be gentlemanly to Agnes, whom Mother had asked to share in the celebration.

"Charles, you'll be a wonderful policeman," Charles's mother said, beaming broadly, "and, Agnes, you look beautiful tonight. Charles is fortunate to have your company on this enchanted evening."

Badge couldn't help but wonder if his mother was hallucinating. Agnes had doubled in size since high school, and he smiled inwardly as he mused, "Christ, anything that ugly has to have cobwebs in her snatch."

"Father, let's be off so we can leave these two young people to ponder their future," Badge's mother said grandly as Agnes smiled awkwardly.

Wordlessly, his father followed his mother to the exit.

Badge then forced a smile and said, "Mother was right, Agnes. You do look lovely tonight." Inside, however, he was thinking, *Well, at least you're not a baby hippo anymore—now you're full-grown.*

Martin and Chimlyn did what needed to be done to graduate. They were typically naïve teenagers, thinking their lives were full of endless tomorrows with limitless possibilities. They couldn't know that an older person was looming in their future—one who would torment them with lies and deceit. Concealed behind a badge, that man would wipe away their youthful smiles and crush their boyish optimism.

—CHAPTER 2—

GIRLS
"Amazed" (Lonestar)

Robin was well thought of and heavily sought-after. All the boys wanted her, like dogs want raw meat. She had laughing eyes and sweet laughter that sent boys into the stratosphere.

Boys longed for the rush provided by her smile and desired her attention, but many a would-be suitor found his words sticking on his tonsils or his tongue being twisted around the syllables as he tried to speak to her. Her beauty turned boys into mumbling, stumbling idiots.

"Christ, she's too good for you," friends would tell Chimlyn. "I mean, check her out!"

Chimlyn knew that he had been born at night—but not the night before, so he'd just reply, "Ah, she's just kinda good-lookin', and for now, that's all I'm doin'—just lookin'."

In truth, Chimlyn didn't need anyone to tell him he wasn't good enough for Robin. Her folks owned a store and were important businesspeople. Chimlyn was just a farm kid, outfitted in garage sale clothes. Ma always said they weren't dirt poor, but to Chimlyn, it felt like they were living on hot air and rabbit tracks.

When someone would joke, "Chicks like Robin don't get laid every day—they get laid every other day," Chimlyn laughed—not because he got the joke, but to fit in.

One weekend, a miracle happened, and Chimlyn got a chance to talk to Robin—but it was only because Robin thought it was cool that he played football. Robin was a cheerleader and sports guys were the only ones who ever stood a chance with her. To everyone's amazement, Robin took a liking to Chimlyn, and his life would never be the same.

Suddenly, Chimlyn loved life and was even starting to enjoy school. Robin made it easy to love everything around him, and although Chimlyn hated birds and considered them flying shit factories, Robin had one for a pet—a parrot named Peachy that could talk.

Chimlyn acted as if he thought Peachy was special, but Robin had her doubts. She'd remind Chimlyn how important it was for him to get along with Peachy if he and she were ever going to have a future together. After all, African Greys could live for seventy years and Peachy was only five.

The one time Chimlyn tried to feed the yellow-eyed bird a sunflower seed, he got nipped on the finger. It didn't really hurt and his scream was out of proportion to any pain felt, so Chimlyn felt stupid for acting like such a baby.

"Birds are unpredictable and you have to exercise caution around them. Peachy is a male and they can be aggressive," Robin said as Chimlyn licked his injured finger.

"Robin," Chimlyn said tentatively, "I hope Peachy will get more used to me after spending more 'quality time' with me," but he wasn't sure that was going to be the case—especially if the damned bird bit him again.

When Chimlyn got his driver's license after taking the written part of the test four times, he got to see Robin even more. He took her to both the junior and senior proms and a physical relationship developed, involving lots of kissing and making out. He knew the priests always barked about the wages of sin and that God had quite a temper, so Chimlyn tried hard not to break his laws—but he was glad when Robin assured him that God wouldn't punish them for making out.

Chimlyn loved Robin—and her body.

She told him, "I'm saving my virginity for you. How does that make you feel, buster?"

"I, uh, feel good," he stammered. "Yeah, pretty good, I suppose."

Robin smiled as they went back to making out. For his part, Chimlyn had Robin, his virginity, and a Plymouth Road Runner—but he only wanted two of those things.

As Lacy passed Martin on the Commons, he walked smack-dab into a light pole, so she knew he was checking her out. How else could anyone walk into a pole?

"Are you okay?" she asked, turning around and trying not to laugh. "You clocked that pole pretty good."

"Uh, yeah," Martin said, brushing himself off and trying to recover come of his dignity. "I about knocked myself silly."

"Here, let me help you pick up your books," offered Lacy.

"Thanks," Martin said, regaining some of his composure. "If you're a nursing student, that would be good, coz I'm feeling a little woozy. Can I buy you lunch—coffee, pop, whatever? I know it was kinda stupid to walk into a pole like that. How about it?"

"I have a class right now, but I'll see ya around," Lacy said, turning to walk away. Then she called over her shoulder. "Watch out for those poles—oh, and I'm in Elementary Ed, not nursing."

As he watched her walk away, Martin wondered if he had any chance with her at all.

Badge's nickname followed him to Normal. He relished every moment spent in his uniform and hated taking days off. Being a cop was as important to him as oxygen, and he walked around holding his stomach in and thrusting his chest out whenever he was in uniform. He had never imagined how great it was going to feel to have people call him "sir." The potential seemed endless.

Badge discovered that working the night shift was his ticket to paradise. Parks closed long before bars did. Badge watched couples park and then gave them time to get naked before approaching the vehicle. He relished seeing as much tit and ass as possible as clothes were hurriedly being thrown back on.

Hookers were his specialty. He knew their language and amazed his superiors with his ability to bust them. Luscious Lucia had cost him a pretty penny, but he took all her lessons to heart.

He'd make sure to gargle with beer before showing up at a motel door in plain clothes and saying, "Yeah, baby, let's party."

When a hooker asked, "Honey, what kinda party you all want?" he couldn't bring up the issue of money. That was a no-no. The courts called it entrapment.

Instead, he would say, "Oh, I was thinking about a little missionary and finishing up in the backdoor."

"That gonna cost ya one fifty."

"Green apples...green apples," Badge would mummer into the concealed microphone in his shirt pocket—a code to bring uniformed officers storming into the room to make the arrest.

After the woman was dragged off to jail, Badge would stick around to collect evidence, one of the duties he loved to perform alone. He'd count the used condoms in the trash and be flooded with desire as his libido shifted into overdrive.

He also enjoyed the sights and smells of lingerie. He loved police work that provided him with opportunities to satisfy the Urge by stimulating it with a pair of pink panties. That was a bonus for the boner. He'd fondle the pink garment, touching himself until he was pulled into depths of wanderlust and wouldn't stop until his desire was released all over them. Then he'd hurriedly put everything back into proper cop order.

Badge became proficient at waiting until a whore was naked and he was down to his underwear. That was perfect: making arrests and feeding the Urge, like eating his cake and having it to. He even started collecting pink intimate apparel and took great pleasure in his private collection. Pink came in many different shades and accents. Nights drifted by, and before he knew it he'd be rummaging in another hooker's underwear drawer after sending her to jail.

"Don't know how you do it, Badge, his lieutenant told him. "You've sure got a knack for busting hookers. You're a natural crime fighter."

It wasn't long until Badge was made a sergeant.

Chimlyn did well enough at stomping gridiron opponents to garner attention from Mankato State, which was just up the road a spell from Madelia. His life continued to revolve around football, farm work, and Robin, who still worked in her parents' store. Everything was working out perfectly—and then it happened, during his first game as a Mankato State Maverick.

Agnes had found a job providing tours of Minnesota's State Capitol building. She was always polite and conservatively dressed at a time when most other young women were running around in practically nothing. Agnes viewed her job as a sacred duty.

Agnes was to be in attendance at what was supposed to be Badge's promotion party at the delicatessen, but Badge's mother made the real reason for the get together clear to him. "I raised you to be a fine, upstanding young man. All I want is what's best for you."

"But, Mother, I know that Agnes is very nice and a proper young lady, but I just don't love—"

"I will not hear this!" Mother interrupted, tears beginning to roll down her cheeks.

Hoping to end the tearful display, Badge said softly, "Well, Mother, I was going to surprise you both by asking Agnes to marry me, but—"

This time Badge's words just trailed off. He simply couldn't bring himself to finish the sentence. All he could hope was that Agnes would turn him down.

"Oh, my!" Agnes said happily when Badge finally summoned the courage during the evening to pop the question. "I'd be honored to marry you, Charles."

Badge tried to look happy, but he just sat in stunned silence as Agnes threw her arms around him in a joyous embrace. It was as if he was floating above his body. In his mind, he could almost hear the jokes that the guys from the chip factory would be telling about him.

"I don't think I could even get it up with a crane for that."

"Christ, they couldn't brew enough beer to bang an oinker like that."

"She's a real two-bagger. You'd haveta slip two bags over her head in case one ripped."

"Yeah, she's a buffarilla, that's for sure. Living proof that a buffalo can fuck a gorilla."

Charles and Agnes had never had any meaningful discussions about how they would coexist as man and wife. He had assumed she was frigid as an iceberg, and she was confused and clueless about men. As far as she was concerned, Charles had never seemed to possess any of the baser instincts. He had always acted like a perfect gentleman.

In her bridal gown, Agnes looked—well, like Agnes. There were very few comments about what a beautiful bride she was. The best people would remember about the wedding was that everything was nice and that Charles and Agnes seemed to be happy.

Agnes even expressed concern about whether the governor was coming to the wedding or not. Although Badge thought it was ridiculous, he kept his thoughts to himself, even though Agnes truly seemed to think it was a possibility. To Agnes's dismay, the governor never showed. Apparently tour guides didn't warrant his time.

As Charles walked down the aisle, filled with pain and humiliation, his mother smiled approvingly. As painful as it was, he couldn't have Mother being unhappy. It simply wasn't acceptable.

When he arrived at the altar of doom, he couldn't even look at Agnes. Instead, he found some momentary relief in checking out the maid of honor's cleavage. The voice of the priest finally pulled him back to grim reality.

"Do you, Charles Paul Pullet..."

When the priest had finished asking the fatal question, Badge found himself incapable of choking out the official words. "I—I—yes, yes." He never did manage to say, "I Do."

In the audience, his mother leaned over to her husband and whispered, "Isn't that nice? Our son is getting all choked up. I told you this was the right idea."

For his part, Badge's father simply nodded in silence as he shook his head sadly.

At the reception, Mother let everyone know that she had taken care of the honeymoon arrangements. "I set them up at a resort on Mackinac Island. I even paid for them to see the island in a horse-drawn carriage. It was expensive, but your son only gets married once—but I let them know they can thank me by presenting me with several perfect grandchildren. You should have seen them blush!"

The wedding picture-taking process was uncomfortable, and it was made even worse by the fact that the photographer assumed

Charles and Agnes actually loved each other. The pictures that resulted weren't something anyone would have wanted to see later. Lacy garters lose all their sex appeal when they're wrapped around a short, swollen, hippopotamus-like leg. Charles and Agnes kissed for only the second time (the first was during the wedding ceremony) because the photographer insisted.

Though she kept it to herself, Agnes was concerned about how she would fare on the honeymoon night. She knew that Charles, being a man, would have designs involving her body. Her concern eventually began to manifest itself in severe stomach pain.

"Oh, dear," Charles's mother said, "I hope it's not appendicitis."

Brant, Agnes's father, assured her, "No, I'm sure she's just nervous. Lots of things going on in that young girl's head."

When they finally got away from the reception, Badge was on his best behavior during the drive to Mackinac. He was even considerate enough to pick up some Pepto-Bismol for Agnes.

"Thank you for being so thoughtful, Charles," she said as he kept his eyes glued to the road ahead.

Badge smiled and patted her on the shoulder, and though Agnes found it comforting, what Badge was really thinking was, "Yeah, I like that pink color—especially in lacy panties."

While Agnes was laid up in the hotel room nursing her aching stomach, Badge was able to indulge the Urge. While she was moaning, he was roaming. As he walked the beaches to enjoy bitches, he reveled in impure thoughts for all the other women he saw.

He got rock hard at the sight of women sitting beside the hotel pool—until Agnes surprised him by showing up, which immediately tore down his trouser tent. Even so, he clung tenaciously to his dirty thoughts as he watched a beautiful young girl pull the back of her bikini bottom out of the crack of her butt.

There were more than enough scantily clad women to make

Badge's honeymoon memorable as he lingered by the poolside, his hard-on carefully hidden inside his baggy swimwear. He also wore mirrored sunglasses to conceal the direction his eyes were looking.

As time went on, nobody knew what he was like on the inside—including Agnes. The truth was always kept carefully hidden. Badge and Agnes eventually bought a house in Normal.

Badge was never able to adequately explain why he had to marry Agnes. He was embarrassed to tell people that his mother had forced him to do it. He was also unable to tell anyone that he knew with all his heart that he was allowing his mother to destroy his life.

"Oh, come on. You a cop? Really?" Lacy asked, her eyes sparkling as they sat together in a restaurant. "You'll have to quit walking into poles, you know."

As she took a bite of her sub sandwich, Martin realized that Lacy could say anything she wanted and he'd always feel better.

"Well, what makes you think you're schoolteacher material?" he asked playfully.

Once upon a time, Martin had been the type of guy to fall head over heels in lust at the drop of a dime. He liked to think that he had deposited enough rubbers on a certain secluded stretch of road to cause road graders to get stuck.

However, although Martin had spent many hours at lover's lane, he had never arrived at love's true destination. It would take years of struggle, combined with just the right amount of luck, for him to walk into a pole—and into his true heart's desire.

Lacy led Martin to places he'd never been before—places like being totally in the moment and wanting nothing but to be in her presence. He knew that he'd rather be with Lacy in her worst mood than any other girl at her best. His desire spread completely across Universe Martin, and public displays of affection were the norm.

"Dude, do you wanna get blasted tonight? I'm talking beer bongs," Jay asked, hoping it was an offer his friend couldn't refuse.

"No. I'm taking Lacy out for pizza," Martin replied. "Then we'll pick up a movie or something."

"Fuck, man," Jay whined. "You're getting pussy whipped. How can ya blow off beer bongs? You're losing it, dude, I'm tellin' ya."

Later that night, Martin stumbled over the words, but finally managed to say, "Come on, Lacy, just marry me, will ya please?"

He had picked up pizza and a chick flick, and had taped the engagement ring to the DVD cover.

With tears in her eyes, Lacy whispered, "Yes."

Lacy was all about the nobler things in life—laughing, dreaming, and the goodness of people. She liked Martin's confident attitude, but he was an enigma to her at times. He was too loud sometimes and always thought he was funny, yet he had gotten teary-eyed as he asked her to marry him.

On the day of the wedding, Martin went to confession. When he was done, he was ready to receive the holy sacrament of marriage.

Lacy looked stunning in her white gown and veil, and Martin had absolutely no problem saying "I Do" three times in succession, simply because he loved the way the words made him feel. The day was filled with happiness and both Martin and Lacy were radiant as they strolled out of the church into the next chapter of their lives—as man and wife.

While opening wedding presents the next day with friends and family, they graciously accepted the usual crock pots and gift certificates, but the biggest surprise had arrived in the mail. It was an offer for Martin to pursue his dream job in a town south of the Twin Cities. Neither Martin nor Lacy knew anything about the city, but they were eager to find out more. The job offer was extended on the condition that he could pass a physical and mental evaluation.

The name of the town was Normal.

After a honeymoon in Minneapolis, they got ready to move. It was exciting and their joy was unrestrained. There was no way for them to know that something dark was waiting for them in Normal—something that would soon put an end to that happiness.

—CHAPTER 3—

TILL DEATH DO US PART
"Hey There Delilah" (Plain White T's)

Everything was set. Robin and her family had met Chimlyn's family (along with a beaming Uncle Lobs) at Blakeslee Stadium in Mankato. Robin couldn't understand why Chimlyn was so bent on playing football, but she had to admit it was exciting.

They picked up a program and looked up Chimlyn's name. He was a defensive tackle and his hometown was listed as Madelia. Robin was proud of what Chimlyn had managed to do. It was as if he had put Madelia on the map. It all seemed like big time stuff.

The Mavericks were dressed in purple. The stadium held 7,000 people and the place was packed. The school's marching band was playing—much better than Madelia's high school band. The weather was perfect for football. Some of the male students were wearing no shirts and had the top half of their bodies painted purple. It was much different from high school football.

Robin liked Lobs. Looking at him with a smile, she asked, "How come you're not painted purple?"

Lobs just smiled and beamed with pride for his nephew. Life was good.

After kicking off, the La Crosse Eagles held the Mavericks to no gain, forcing them to punt. The entire family cheered as Chimlyn trotted onto the field.

Robin watched in horror as Chimlyn was knocked down on the very first play and lay motionless on the field as the medical staff ran out to check on him. A hush fell over the crowd as the team doctor called for a stretcher. No one knew quite what was going on, but rumors circulated that it had something to do with his back.

The families had to pile into cars for a trip to the Immanuel St. Joseph hospital, a short distance from the stadium. During the entire drive, no one spoke.

After an examination, a doctor came into the waiting room and told the families that Chimlyn had suffered a herniated disk. He explained that spinal injuries could be tricky, but Chimlyn hadn't sustained any injury to his spinal cord. After some rest, accompanied by pain and anti-inflammatory medications, and some physical therapy, the prognosis was good.

The families then quickly headed for Chimlyn's room. He told them that he had gotten caught up with two blockers who then had driven him over another guy. He felt pain shoot through his legs and couldn't move without the pain getting much worse.

"I hollered, but those guys kept driving into me!" he explained. "They wouldn't stop."

Luckily, Chimlyn hadn't lost any feeling in his legs, which the doctor said was great news. However, the doctor did say that there were a lot of unknowns when it came to back injuries. He might be able to play without any problems—or he might end up hurting his back even worse. Reluctantly, Chimlyn resigned himself to the fact that he probably wouldn't be playing any more football.

An inner voice told him, "You're too scared to play with those bastards! What are you going to do if you mess your back up worse, ask Robin to wipe your ass for you?"

Chimlyn had to drop out of school, since it was hard to stay in college when he couldn't even sit up. Robin began hanging out at his house. He and Robin became very close and he relied on her judgment. She assured him that she was going to help make him all better again.

Chimlyn couldn't believe he'd been just an average-sized player in college. He had no idea there were so many guys bigger and meaner than he was. He hated the thought of being a chicken shit, but he hated the back pain even worse.

Since his football days were over, he wondered if he should even stay in college. He was lost. He didn't want to admit that he'd never step onto a football field again. Would people know that he could have played but was too afraid? Maybe he was too much like his dad— mild-mannered and scared to death of being hurt. What would Lobs think of him?

Football wasn't just a game to Chimlyn. It was an escape from reality. When he was playing, everyone wanted what he had—but that had suddenly become a thing of the past.

"Chimlyn, you might never walk again if you try to play football," Robin said tearfully. "Football shouldn't be more important than me."

Robin felt bad for Chimlyn but she also knew they still could have a great future together. She had supported him when he wanted to play football, but she prayed secretly that he would come to realize that his playing days were over.

When a person is forced by circumstances to embrace their limitations and face their fears, a wise person realizes that they'll never live up to their original promise. At that moment, it's time to cut back on expectations and to seek a different direction, even if it means facing a life of simply punching a clock, eating, sleeping, and then punching that same clock again.

Love is the binding that holds it all together. Chimlyn was fortunate to have the kindness and concern of a loving woman. He had Robin to be his reason for quitting football.

Even so, there were times when he found himself thinking, "I was *somebody* at Madelia High. I was kick ass on the football field and I was respected. I got to go to the Barn when I was a freshman."

Yet it had all slipped away, and now it was time to make other plans. Where were all the things he had taken for granted—friends, teachers, and everything else that had once been the center of his universe? They had suddenly disappeared and wouldn't be coming back.

His back hurt unbearably if he twisted a certain way, and Chimlyn became dependent on Robin. She was so much more than a girlfriend. She was his life's meaning and his future, and he relied on Robin to try to make sense out of a world gone mad.

Robin continued working in her parents' store, the Ben Franklin, and was content with her lot in life. She's never felt any pull that would take her away from Madelia. Her family provided her with a livelihood, combined with a safe and secure environment. She loved the order her life provided, and she was satisfied.

"Honey, are you always going to be a small town girl?" her dad asked one day. "Are you sure you want to keep this store afloat? Walmart and Kmart are making it tougher on everyone."

When her dad said such things, she knew in her heart that he was probably right, but she assured him, "We'll be okay, Dad. Folks will always need what we have."

The inevitability of change annoyed her at times. Why couldn't things just stay the same so she could just work hard and live well in

Madelia? She'd seen her dad and mom do it over the years. Why wasn't there a way a person could fight the changing times?

One day, she admitted to her mom, "I hate to say it, but with that new Walmart just down the road, there's a lot of stuff we carry that people can buy cheaper there."

When Highway 169 was made into a four-lane road, it bypassed Madelia but went right by Walmart south of town and Kmart not too far north. "Oh, the times they are a-changin'," Bob Dylan sang on MTV, a new station people could see on cable. Where had the Partridge Family gone?

Robin wondered about such things, and she also wondered how Chimlyn was going to deal with those changes. He hung around the store after his back started getting better and did his best to be helpful. She liked how he put so few demands on her and always tried to do whatever she asked without complaint.

It was comforting to know that he wasn't interested in chasing around and drinking. He was always with her in church on Sunday. He seemed to be logical, kind of like the store. She went through the passing seasons, putting up displays, making sales, and paying the bills. It just seemed logical for her to marry Chimlyn and have a safe, predictable life. Other girls her age were already married. It all made perfect sense to her.

One day, she tried to gently persuade Chimlyn to apply at the Tony Downs poultry plant. "You'd do well there," she said. "It pays good and they have benefits—and since you never liked birds, you'd be getting a chance to dispose of thousands of them."

She laughed at her little joke, but Chimlyn had never even considered working in a factory, standing in a windowless building all day. After all, he'd been brought up as a farm boy, amid wide open fields. He conveniently forgot that he had never been much of a farm boy and that his back probably would never let him do farm work again, even if he wanted to.

"Naw," Chimlyn said. "I'll figure something out, though, don't ya worry about that. I'll do right by you, and that's a fact, Jack."

Chimlyn then laughed as if he didn't have a care in the world, but he was hiding behind his laughter. What was he *really* going to do with his life?

For her part, Robin was careful not to let Chimlyn know he was irritating her, thinking, "What he doesn't know won't hurt him."

As the winter days passed, Chimlyn was finally pronounced fit as a fiddle, which made him even more aware that he was going to have to make some decisions regarding his future. Lobs had mentioned something that sounded interesting. (Actually, most things Lobs said were interesting to Chimlyn.)

"Just between you, me, and the pissing post," Lobs said, "I think you'd make a better-than-average truck driver. You'd be your own boss, driving one of them big rigs all over the country. You could get set up in New Ulm. There's a couple big companies over there. None of that being locked up in one place the rest of your life. All ya need is a Class A license and you're on the road to success!"

Chimlyn nodded and said, "Yeah, it wouldn't hurt to check it out, I guess."

The next day, Chimlyn headed down Highway 15 toward New Ulm—a new town and a new direction in life. After flunking the written driver's test on his first attempt, he began practicing for the road test part by driving grain trucks around the farm. If he didn't understand something, Lobs helped. That part was much easier for him.

The next week, he took the written test a second time—but flunked again. He was frustrated, but more determined than ever.

On the third try, he finally passed, and he immediately applied at a company in New Ulm. He was excited when they offered him a job on the spot. It all seemed perfect. The work wouldn't bother his back, he'd be making good money, and he wouldn't be working in a poultry processing plant.

What he didn't know was the strain such long distance trucking would put on his relationship with Robin. It wasn't going to be easy to be a loving, devoted family man when he was constantly running across the country with loads of cumquats bound for Timbuktu.

Robin held down the store as best she could, but the competition was fierce, and customers jumped ship to save a few pennies. She started taking night courses at South Central Technical College. She wanted to improve her accounting skills, which her dad thought was a great idea.

"Robin, they can take pretty much anything away from you," her dad said, "but they can't touch your education."

It gave her dad peace of mind to know that his daughter was picking up some education, since he was apprehensive about the direction retailing was headed. Mom and pop stores were rapidly becoming dinosaurs.

Chimlyn knew that he was going to make something out of himself, he would have to work, and truck driving seemed like the logical way to go. Maybe their optimism about their future was due to their youth or the fact that they had grown up in a tiny town, but they honestly believed that better days were coming. For them, life was about doing good things, and the priest always said that God took care of the righteous.

However, the stones of human behavior sometimes smash even the most optimistic hearts into sorry pieces.

Chimlyn and Robin's lives were about goodness and honesty. They had no doubt that God would be there for them when they needed him. They never thought about the fact that the world also contained mean-spirited folks—real people like the ones they saw on cop shows and the nightly news. That kind of stuff happened in other places and to other people. It didn't happen in little ole' Madelia.

Chimlyn was a gentle giant who wouldn't have hurt a cockroach. He wasn't a thoroughbred of speed. He was a plow horse of predictability. He wasn't a great love maker, but he never forgot to get Robin a heart-shaped box of chocolates on Valentine's Day—always the same box of chocolates from the same store.

Once he learned how to do something, he did it the same way—forever. "Why fix something that ain't broke?" Chimlyn would quote Lobs as saying.

Although Robin would act surprised and compliment Chimlyn for being so thoughtful, she had just been thinking, "Come on, Chimlyn, where are you with your heart? We gotta get rolling."

A steady routine can be a good thing, until it becomes mundane. Then it can turn into a mood killer.

In the grand scheme of things, they hadn't spent enough time together to realize that there were things in and about life that should have told them it would be best to say goodbye to each other—so they didn't.

They got married.

"Do you, Chimlyn, take Robin—" the priest droned on as a wide-eyed Chimlyn listened intently, trying to catch every word.

There was an uncomfortable silence when the priest finally finished speaking. Then Chimlyn realized it was his turn to speak, and although he was only expected to say, "I do," he surprised everyone by exclaiming, "Yeah! Yes, I will! I really will!"

After the ceremony, they made a truck run together out to the West Coast, which served as their honeymoon. It wasn't what Robin might have preferred, but at least they were finally married. She wanted to see Las Vegas, and they actually did stop to have a little cookout on the bluffs overlooking Vegas on their way to the coast.

As Chimlyn drove, they talked about the things they saw, and they actually had a nice time spending more time together than they'd ever done in the past. Robin was spellbound by the Pacific Ocean and surprised at how cold it was, even near Salinas, California.

John Steinbeck had grown up in Salinas and wrote about it when it had been a small town. Robin wondered if it had been like Madelia in his day. It certainly wasn't like that anymore.

As they waited in a parking lot for the trailer to be loaded with produce, another trucker joked, "You know how you haul chickens on a flatbed?" When neither Chimlyn or Robin ventured a guess, he said, "You nail their peckers to the floor."

Chimlyn didn't get it, but Robin laughed.

On the way back, they decided to follow the coast north and then swing across the Bay Bridge in San Francisco before heading toward the Sierra Nevada mountains. When they arrived in the Bay Area, the Golden Gate Bridge was shrouded in fog. That had made Chimlyn mad, but there was nothing he could do about it, and Robin made him feel better by gushing about the romantic beauty of the fog over the water.

As they rolled along, the scenery looked even more spectacular than in the picture books. They stopped in Wendover, Nevada, where Robin remarked that there were more lights in the Rainbow Casino than in the entire town of Madelia. The mountains were Robin's favorites though. Having grown up in southern Minnesota, she couldn't get enough of the Sierra Nevada range, the Wasatch mountains, or the Rockies. She was mesmerized by how enormous and beautiful they were.

"Gosh," she exclaimed, "do you think Madelia will ever look the same after we've seen all of this?"

When Chimlyn looked slightly confused by her comment, Robin didn't attempt to explain her feelings. That would have been too difficult—and it might have ruined the mood. They were officially husband and wife, and she was sure that even though they wouldn't always understand each other, they'd stay married forever because they were both good, religious people. They had both grown up in the same town, gone to the same school, and had the same friends. Even with life's uncertainties, they'd be happy because that was what God wanted.

When they got back to Minnesota, they drove to the Twin Cities to unload the truck. Robin found it amazing that Chimlyn could roll such a huge truck into such tight places, but he did.

It would take hours to unload the trailer, so they decided to go for a walk to kill some time. After eating at a Kentucky Fried Chicken, something they couldn't do in Madelia, Chimlyn suggested walking to see a cathedral in St. Paul that was so big that several Madelia churches could easily fit inside. Robin knew Chimlyn didn't make up stories, so she was curious.

When she saw how huge the Cathedral of Saint Paul was, she was again amazed—and unsettled. Up to the moment they had left on their honeymoon run, she had thought Madelia was the center of the universe and all other towns would somehow be similar to Madelia. She'd been to Mankato and thought it was a big city, but she'd never seen anything like the things she'd seen on their trip.

As they looked at the huge edifice, Robin wondered aloud, "Where do they find enough Catholics to fill such a place? Do they have more than one Mass a day?"

After the cathedral, they strolled over the interstate and walked around the State Capitol. Chimlyn had shown her the glass plate photo collection he had of the capitol when it was under construction. It was one of the first things he had shared with her when they first started going out. All that seemed so long ago.

It was a magical time and they laughed from the sheer joy of sharing such an amazing time together. As they approached the front door of the building, an overweight lady asked them what was so funny.

She gave them the impression that she didn't approve of laughter. Her name tag identified her as: Curator/Guide Mrs. Pullet.

"Oh, we're just trying to figure out where some pictures were taken of this place when it was being built, back in horse-and-buggy days," Chimlyn explained.

The woman nodded her head as she said in a well-rehearsed voice, "The construction on this building commenced in 1896 and was completed in 1905." Then she paused and asked, even though she didn't really sound interested, "Where did you see the pictures you're referring to?"

"My husband has a collection of pictures he found on the farm when he was growing up," replied Robin. "They show various stages of construction and they were actually exposed on glass by some primitive method."

For the first time, Mrs. Pullet showed some genuine feeling, her tone becoming more friendly as she asked, "Do tell, young lady. Perhaps it was the collodion process? Is the detail very fine? I would love to see it. I'd even take the time to travel to your residence, if that would be more convenient for you."

She then gave them her phone number. Chimlyn was amazed to see someone who took her job so seriously. He was also surprised to have someone take such an interest in the photographs. He'd only recently picked them up at the farm and brought them to his new home. He wondered if this strange woman would really drive all the way to Madelia to see them.

After saying goodbye to Mrs. Pullet, they headed east toward Hill House, a huge brick mansion built by a railroad tycoon to be an advertisement of his accumulated wealth.

"It makes you wonder how it would feel to be that rich, doesn't it?" Chimlyn asked as they stood in front of the imposing structure, but in his head, he could hear Lobs joke, "Yeah, but you'll see bulls give milk before you ever get that rich."

Even so, pipe dreams are what honeymoons were supposed to be about, and Chimlyn and Robin shared their dreams as their honeymoon came to an end. Robin would soon be going back to work and school while Chimlyn drove his truck.

Robin made Chimlyn promise that they'd never let things get out of hand like Old Man Meyer and his wife had. Just because a couple got old was no reason to stop loving each other.

Robin talked about Mr. Meyer as they headed out of the Twin Cities. "He was old enough to retire, so he sold all his cows. Milking's a lot of work. Then he bought a whole new herd less than a year later. He told his neighbors that milking cows every day was easier than being in the house with his wife. Can you imagine?"

Robin went on and on about how she never wanted that to happen to them, which made Chimlyn happy, because he truly loved her and never wanted to get divorced. After all, God wasn't somebody to mess around with. Chimlyn smiled as he turned the rig onto Highway 169 toward their new life in Madelia. Robin was the best thing that had ever happened to him and he would never do anything to mess it up.

Except for the parrot, Peachy, everything for Chimlyn was, well, peachy. It didn't matter that African grays could live to be seventy years old. Most people's pets didn't live nearly that long. Romille Crawford once had a blue parakeet that flew smack dab into an old-fashioned electric fan and was sliced up, so he knew that birds could sometimes be gone in a heartbeat. He even wondered if he could pick up a couple of big fans for around their new rental house just off the main drag in Madelia. The thought made him smile, but he kept it to himself.

Robin and Chimlyn—what would the future have in store for a young couple so full of hopes and aspirations? Only time would tell.

—CHAPTER 4—

CENTER OF ATTENTION
"You're So Vain" (Carly Simon)

Robin and Chimlyn had no way of knowing that the enormous lady they met at the capitol was married to a police officer in Normal, a town just two hours from Madelia.

Normal was in the process of promoting one of its police officers to lieutenant at its next monthly city council meeting. The community had hired a replacement to fill the vacancy by adding Martin McMurphy, a recent St. Cloud graduate, to the police force. Just married, he had rented a house on the outskirts of town and was looking forward to serving citizens of Normal.

After Martin's wedding, the usual chores were addressed: paying the priest, saying goodbye to relatives, and then packing for the move toward the Iowa border. They were leaving the beautiful middle part of the state and heading for the endless flat fields of corn and soybeans. (People referred to them as cash crops, even though the farmers who grew them always seemed to be complaining. The old joke was that if you put enough grain farmers in a basement, you'd have a "whine cellar.")

It was going to be a big change for the McMurphys, but the pain of the move was lessened by the knowledge that they'd only have to endure the prairie for a year. After that, Martin would be considered an experienced officer and they could choose another area more to their liking.

The ceremonies during the city council meeting were typical small town stuff. Martin felt uncomfortable standing around while a bunch of small town dignitaries strutted around filled with their own imagined self-importance, but he had to meet the city fathers. It was just part of the ritual.

As the evening wore on, Lacy snapped pictures, although Martin couldn't understand why she'd want to waste film on something they'd never want to see again. After the formalities and a brief comment to a reporter from the town's weekly newspaper, Martin finally sat next to Lacy. Now all he had to do was stay awake for the rest of the meeting. He was hoping the meeting would end soon enough for them to hit the local Ace Hardware and then get back home to keep working on making their new home more livable.

As the meeting droned on, Martin made a decision. If anyone ever asked him to get into politics, he wouldn't do it—and especially small town politics. All he wanted to do was get out of that meeting and get on with his life. It was worse than an endless church service.

Instead, he had to act as if he cared about whatever the city finance director was talking about. He felt sorry for that man and the direction he had chosen for his life. His mental ramblings were interrupted as everyone turned in unison and looked toward the back of the room.

In walked a uniformed officer who looked as if he was the happiest man on earth. His hair was perfectly groomed and parted on the side in a style that hadn't been fashionable in more than a decade. His lips were thin, just a crack in his face, but his smile made it clear that he was ecstatic about what was about to happen. This was *his* supreme moment.

He had obviously been primping for a long time to look as spit-and-polished as he did—pants pressed, badge polished, and every buckle and button gleaming. Martin actually found it hard to believe what he was seeing.

Martin leaned over and whispered to his wife, "Have you ever seen anything like that? Do you think all the cops walk around polished up like that?"

Suppressing a giggle, Lacy whispered, "Shush! I'm sure he dressed up special today because he's happy that he's being promoted."

"I hope you're right," Martin whispered, never taking his eyes off the human spectacle that was slowly walking down the aisle of the hall, basking in the crowd's attention.

The chief of police was sitting at the end of the table where the other council members were seated, smiling as proudly as a father watching his son graduate from college.

Martin looked to his left and saw a heavy lady glaring at him disapprovingly. He immediately sat up straight and gave the solemn ceremony his rapt attention. He had to play it cool. He couldn't piss off the locals on his first day. He could only hope she wasn't the mayor's—or worse yet, the police chief's—wife.

He wondered if everyone went through things like what he was experiencing at that moment. He was almost embarrassed to watch little Napoleon waltzing down the aisle, but he quickly put on his professional face before Lacy got a hold of him by the short hairs and made him shape up.

After the ceremonies had been concluded, the newly promoted lieutenant strutted among the crowd of well-wishers, receiving praise and drinking in their adulation. As far as Martin was concerned, it was a pitiful scene, but he pasted on his best smile and began greeting all the people who wanted to welcome Lacy and himself to the community.

Although it seemed like forever, it really wasn't long before the police chief came over and introduced Martin and Lacy to the new lieutenant. "Martin McMurphy and Lacy," he said proudly, "I'd like you to meet Lieutenant Charles Pullet. We call him Badge for short."

While everyone laughed at the nickname, the chief added, "He's a good man with an excellent record and I think the two of you will get along just fine."

As Badge shook hands first with Martin and then with Lacy, the police chief reached out, pulled Badge's mother to his side, and said, "And this is Lieutenant Pullet's mother."

As he shook hands with the woman, Martin couldn't help noticing that she seemed to be the type of person whose nose was constantly pointed toward the sky in a permanent better-than-thou posture.

Then Badge's father was introduced—a balding man with an air of quiet desperation who nodded silently as he shook Martin's hand. Some of Badge's brother and sisters were also introduced, all of them seeming to be much older than Badge.

Finally, to Martin's amazement, the huge woman stepped forward and the police chief introduced her as Badge's wife, Agnes. Before anyone could speak, he then excused himself and left the meeting, leaving Martin and Lacy to fend for themselves.

Agnes giggled somewhat self-consciously and said, using language much too formal for the occasion, "It's been an enchanted evening, to be sure. I'm so pleased that you and all the others afforded yourselves the opportunity to join us in such a happy occasion."

Martin smiled politely, but he was wondering if he had somehow fallen asleep and found himself on a totally different planet. For some reason, an image of Sister Larkin from his grade school days came to mind.

Sister Larkin was an enormous woman, too, and spoke in platitudes, such as, "Waste not, want not. Always remember, dear Martin, that the Lord doesn't approve of throwing food away."

In spite of himself, Martin found himself thinking, "I'll bet this broad cleans her plate up. The Lord must *love* her."

Martin also realized that all the flowery language that was pouring from Agnes's mouth was totally insincere, which made the entire situation seem even more pitiful and bizarre. She was smiling on the outside, but she felt very differently on the inside—of that he was sure. The entire evening was just strange, and he couldn't remember the last time he'd been that uncomfortable.

For Lacy's part, she found herself wondering how Badge's hair had stayed so perfectly in place. After all, it was windy outside. He had to have used half a can of hairspray before heading for the meeting. He seemed to be all about image, carefully choosing his words and even admiring his reflection in the glass of the pictures on the walls from time to time. Was he in love with himself or was he just the proudest new lieutenant in the world?

She actually looked forward to meeting Badge and Agnes again in a more relaxed and normal atmosphere. Knowing how hard Martin had worked to get to that moment, she hoped he would have nice people to work with in his first law enforcement position. First impressions can be way off, she told herself.

Then Lacy received a shock. She caught Badge looking at her in the way a horny guy would. His beady eyes were definitely checking her out, but she let it go. After all, policemen are the good guys. They don't do the horny looking thing.

Even as Agnes continued to ramble, Lacy was trying to comprehend the situation. The new lieutenant was giving her an "I wanna give you wood" look and she saw flashes of repressed anger and frustration in

Agnes's eyes, even as she was laughing. Like Martin, she was uncomfortable, yet she couldn't quite put her finger on why.

A few moments later, she again caught Badge leering at her, but she knew she wouldn't be able to tell Martin about it. They'd be working together and she didn't want to cause any undo friction between them. Even so, she dreaded the inevitable invitation they would receive to spend time alone with Charles Pullet and Agnes.

The party then shifted to Lieutenant Pullet's home, where both Martin and Lacy tried to remain as low-profile as possible. They had promised each other on the way to the house that they'd make an appearance and then dash at the first opportunity.

Interestingly, they discovered that everyone was friendlier when Agnes was not around. They just seemed to be more relaxed, open, and talkative.

Although Martin's aim had been to simply blend in, he should have known that he was going to stand out like a bikini in church. He was the new guy on the block and the entire town was interested in him and his lovely wife. In a small town, every newcomer needed to be examined closely before a judgment could be rendered.

As the night wore on, Martin and Lacy kept smiling, greeting strangers, and trying to say the right things. Eventually they got separated, and Martin found himself trying to make small talk with Agnes.

"I can't believe how nice your husband looked this evening," Martin said, trying to be civil enough that she wouldn't be prompted to tell him exactly why she'd glared at him during the meeting. "How long has your husband been with the Normal police department? You must be very proud of him."

After Agnes had said something that Martin couldn't quite hear over the noisy gathering, he said, "I went to St. Cloud State. Where did you and your husband go, and where did the name Badge come from?"

"We never went to college, Mr. McMurphy," Agnes replied flatly. "We're not even sure that college graduates should be on the force because they're generally looking for trouble and think they know it all." Martin noticed that the flowery language had disappeared as she added, "And I would prefer to have my husband addressed as Lieutenant Pullet."

Martin began to have the sort of sinking feeling guys in the old Tarzan movies must have felt when they suddenly found themselves standing in quicksand. He desperately wished he knew where Lacy was.

As Martin stood in paralyzed silence, a miracle happened—Lacy appeared at his side.

"Oh, there you are, Martin," she said with a smile. "Mrs. Pullet, you have a right to be proud of your husband—but you've had some accomplishments of your own! Your husband was just telling me some of the things you've accomplished during your time as curator at the state capital."

Agnes smiled broadly and said, "It really is an honor to be entrusted with our heritage and to work closely on projects that will insure our legacy."

Martin smiled. The pomp and elegance of her speech was back. She was the consummate phony, and Martin disliked phonies more than just about any other type of person. From that moment on he knew that any day without Agnes in it was going to be a better day.

Talking about her job reminded Agnes that she had misplaced the names and addresses of the couple with the glass plates she'd wanted to see. She was angry that her husband's stupid promotion had been distracting her from her own work. She hated the fact that he had made her move to a worthless town and had taken her away from her important duties at the capitol. His work paled in comparison to hers.

Lacy had her doubts about Badge. He was disingenuous. There was just something wrong with him. She wanted to be wrong for Martin's sake, but Badge rubbed her the wrong way and she was determined to keep him at arm's length.

When they were finally able to escape the party, Lacy told Martin on the way home, "You know, I just didn't feel completely right about tonight. Something just wasn't right."

"Well, color my balls purple and call me gay!" Martin said with a laugh. "You, too?"

Lacy hated it when he talked like that, but she decided to ignore it for the moment.

Before she could say anything, Martin added, "I was standing there, trying to make small talk with Mrs. Lieutenant Black Angus Agnes, and she just went off about how college graduates don't belong in the department. Then, just as I was about to run screaming into the night, you showed up and saved my ass. I owe you a big one for that—thanks."

Then he looked over, gave her a playful wink, and said, "So, baby, what kinda loving do you want tonight? You name it. I've been a bad boy. You want to spank my butt?"

Lacy laughed and gave him a playful punch on the shoulder. It never ceased to amaze her how adept he was at turning a conversation toward sex.

"Don't call Agnes a cow," Lacy finally said. "It makes you sound so juvenile."

They were both glad to be home and they skipped cleaning for the night so they could go straight to bed. When Martin thought about how far he'd come since meeting Lacy, he gave thanks to the Lord. There was no more Mr. Intoxication on the weekends and his mom had to drink alone without scaring the piss out of her frightened son. Sure, the new situation was strange, but it beat the hell out of where he'd been not all that long ago—and they would only need to stick it out for a year. Then his ticket would be punched and they could hit the road for anywhere they wanted to go.

Agnes wasn't happy with everything that had happened that night. She was especially annoyed that the police chief had chosen to leave the meeting and hadn't even showed up for the party afterward. She also didn't like the idea of Charles discussing her job with that new know-it-all officer and his skinny wife. She couldn't believe she'd married someone dumb enough to want to be a police officer—and now he'd been promoted. It all seemed so impossible.

She sat in the living room and wolfed down two leftover sandwiches, washing them down with enormous gulps of punch. She had put too much 7-Up in it, so she belched loudly before downing another sandwich and headed toward the bedroom, picking up various scraps of food and stuffing them into her mouth as she walked. Food always made her feel better, reminding her of the warm comfort of her childhood kitchen and how much easier times were then.

"Was there something wrong with the sandwiches tonight?" she asked Badge as she walked into the bedroom. "Hardly anyone touched the chicken salad. Charles, are you listening to me?"

"Have a pizza or something if you think the chicken is spoiled, dear," Badge suggested blankly. "I gotta go get Tanner. He's been outside all night."

When Badge returned, Agnes said, "Charles, you caused me to lose some important names tonight. I had to run home and put this party together, and now the names are gone. A couple had some pictures of the capitol when it was under construction, and I need those pictures to insure a part of Minnesota's legacy."

When Charles failed to respond, Agnes sighed deeply and said, "Well, if you're not going to talk to me, I'm just going to bed."

When they first moved to town, Agnes had insisted on keeping her capitol job, even though it didn't pay enough to justify keeping it, especially when gas and time were factored in. Yet nothing seemed to make Agnes happy. She could have been the prettiest girl in the world and Charles still would have kept his distance. The ugliness that poured out of that woman was unbelievable—which made Lacy even more attractive in Badge's eyes.

Finally, Badge replied, "Look, Agnes, I'm sorry about the names. I'll help you find them, okay? Let's be friends and call it a night. I'm beat."

Badge sat on the edge of the bed petting Tanner, their golden retriever, who was more than simply a pet, something that often happened with childless couples. Since Tanner got no exercise, she had become as obese in her canine way as Agnes was in a human way—but there was a difference. Badge loved Tanner but not Agnes.

Over the years Agnes had retreated into the relative safety of their small house, her stomach problems, and food. All day, Agnes stood and looked out the small kitchen window, usually nibbling on a little something, counting the minutes until her police officer slipped back into her clutches. He would walk in, sit down, and bobble-head responses to whatever she was rambling about—and she could ramble about everything and everybody, starting with the neighbors and what they were up to. After she grew weary of the neighborhood gossip, she expanded her bitching to include things she saw on television, read in the newspaper, or heard on the radio.

All of that would have been maddening to most men, but Badge wasn't like most men. He had to be perfect, and Agnes had been thrust upon him by his mother. If it hadn't been for Agnes, Mother probably would have worried herself to death—and Badge never would have been able to forgive himself.

Agnes had always had stomach problems, to the point that Badge actually started to grow concerned about her. She moped around the house, usually too sick even to go for walks with him in the afternoon.

He remembered how bad they had been on their honeymoon. She'd been forced to stay in their hotel room most of the time and ate only plain turkey sandwiches. In fact, it seemed like any time they were invited somewhere or to do anything, she'd come down with one of her attacks and be unable to leave the house. It was confusing. She'd be doing well and then, if he were, say, thinking about going out with the guys and their wives—nothing big, just hanging out—bang, she'd have one of her attacks.

If she did let him attend a function without making him feel guilty, he always had to leave before anyone else. He'd also make a point of bringing her a gallon of ice cream—any flavor, as long as it had choco-late in it. The ice cream seemed to help her stomach, because after she had eaten a large helping, her stomach pains improved dramatically.

That was their routine. He hung out and bowled or whatever while Agnes was home suffering. She had his cell phone number, so she could get a hold of him wherever he was.

He tried to get her to see a doctor about it, saying, "I have good insurance with the city, and it might be something they can take care of in a snap," but Agnes clung tenaciously to the security of her illness and refused to go.

Charles Pullet's routine included keeping his hair meticulously groomed. He loved his thick head of hair. His mother had showed him how to comb his hair, and he stuck with the first style she had ever picked for him. He'd never even considered changing it, because he was sure people would laugh and point out the change.

He also took great care of the thing he loved more dearly than any-thing in the world: his badge. He polished his badge every night before dinner and would inspect it again in the morning before heading to work. He loved huffing a misty breath onto it and then rubbing it as he looked at his reflection in the shiny metal. He had no idea why anyone would work in a profession that didn't involve a uniform and a badge. It was certainly the sweetest thing in his life to don his superhero outfit and venture out into the world.

He was relieved that he wasn't getting thin on top like other guys his age. At church he almost had to wear sunglasses to dull the glare off the tops of the heads of the bald men at mass. He had no idea what he would do without his hair, and seeing all those bald men scared him to death.

Badge was ready and willing to be recognized as an authority figure. It made him feel important. He was everything he always wanted to be. He was on TV, in the newspapers, and on the radio. People no longer looked through him, and they actually listened to what he had to say.

Being able to leave Agnes alone with her frustration and loneliness was another reason Badge loved his job. He was able to escape that bitching reminder of what a miserable little boy he really was inside. He paid a high price for the air of perfection he was forced to maintain.

He didn't stop busting hookers or searching out parkers to satisfy the Urge, and Badge was a hands-on type of leader. He loved getting his hands on hookers. He dropped whatever he was doing to assist in any police calls involving sex. He also stayed on the night shift, even after earning enough seniority to jump onto days. When he stepped away from his sexless marriage, his position as an officer put him smack dab in the middle of sexual escapades.

"Now, ma'am, please calm down. Would you like a glass of water? I need you to go over the penetration part again, and do it slowly so I can document it for the court. Don't be embarrassed. I'm a professional, and I've heard it all before."

He loved hearing stories that contained words like *ejaculated semen* and *breasts*.

"Did the man fondle your breasts while penetrating you? What position did he use? It's important that I, I mean we, know how he had sex with you. We must establish his modus operandi."

"Well, he propped me up on all fours and said he'd hurt me if I didn't let him."

Doggie style. Badge wondered why Luscious Lucia always charged him more for his favorite position.

He was always commended for his tireless pursuit of sex offenders and for his thorough reports. His subordinates also took note of how impeccable his uniform was and made jokes in private about his loving his uniform so much that he probably slept in it. Nobody could argue with the fact that Badge loved his job.

It was easier for Badge to be a perfect son when he lived many miles away from his overbearing mother. When she called, he was always on top of his deceitful game.

"Yes, Agnes and I are hoping to get pregnant."

"Yes, we'd love to come up for nephew Bauer's first communion. He's such a sweet boy. I know the Lord will provide us with a little one to call our own someday."

Meanwhile, he was thinking, "Fat chance. I'll die before I impregnate that ugly thing I'm married to."

Agnes never worried about Badge's child-making lies to his mother. As far as she was concerned, he was her perfect little eunuch, and she was happy not to have to put up with that part of being married. Badge didn't seem to need it and she certainly didn't. After being married to him awhile, she learned that the things he told his mother were meant to keep her in line. He survived by being untruthful.

It was at work that Badge was happiest. He was a natural. He even showed up on his days off to have coffee with the chief. He loved to do extra tasks around the department while other cops headed home to loving wives and kids. There was nothing at home for him but misery and regret.

He dreaded the end of each work day, and especially the last day before he was scheduled to be off for a couple of days. It was like being pushed into a gloomy dungeon.

He'd go to the grocery store and then home to Home Sweet Hell. They'd eat a meal and discuss anything deemed interesting by his tormentor. After doing the dishes, she'd plop down in front of the TV and stare in silence while he read his paperback police stories. It was the best he could do to escape from her. He loved reading about sex offenders, rapists, and whores. He was rescued from his dreary existence by the power of the badge and sex crimes.

"Are you reading more police stuff? Can't you ever read anything else?" Agnes would say sarcastically on her way to the kitchen for another bowl of ice cream. "You should try one of the bars I made this afternoon. If you like them, I'll make some for Bauer's communion. Are you listening, Charles?"

Badge couldn't believe how she could get herself all worked up over nothing. After being married for what seemed like an eternity, he knew what to ignore and what to acknowledge with a nod of his head or a subtle grunt. He was good at avoiding arguments, preferring to let her keep running on until she ran out of gas.

Change is inevitable. People, places, and the very fabric of life are constantly being assaulted by the forces of change. Nothing lasts forever, not even the strongest desires that make up the keystones of our lives. Likes, dislikes, tastes, and prejudices are constantly evolving.

Living for the present with fond memories of the past and fears about what tomorrow will bring is ingrained in the human mind. People change and become a newer version of what they had been. Today's consequences are unveiled in the days to come.

Time was rolling on in both Madelia and Normal, and the process of change was marching relentlessly onward. To err is human, and there are some who learn from their mistakes. Other people feed their own diabolical desires by taking advantage of the mistakes of others—and someone was getting hungry, really hungry, in Normal.

—CHAPTER 5—

COPS
"Bad Boys" (Inner Circle)

Lacy and Martin finally got their rental house in order. Normal wasn't a college town, which meant lower rent. They were happy and excited to start life as a married couple.

As far as Martin was concerned, love had a heart, a soul, and a name: Mrs. Lacy McMurphy. Married life was as natural for him as breathing. For him, their anniversaries would always be celebrations of sincere gratitude. She enriched his life and gave him happiness.

On their first morning in Normal, Lacy made Martin's favorite breakfast: biscuits and gravy, delivered in bed. To his surprise, they were too salty, but Martin played the "they're great" game because he knew she had made them with love.

Lacy was driven by a desire to teach grade-schoolers, and she had discovered during her student teaching that she excelled at it. She had never forgotten what her own grade school teachers had meant in her life and hoped to be able to return the favor to a new generation, but she also loved her husband. So when he took the job in Normal, she went along, temporarily postponing her dreams. She put Martin first and she knew he put her first, so their love grew stronger from day to day.

Lacy checked into positions in the Normal school system and surrounding areas, and discovered that Grand Meadow was hiring paraprofessionals. It wasn't a full-time teaching position, but it would allow her to work with children. Grand Meadow was about a half hour away, but she would have driven twice as far for the chance to pursue her dream.

When she pulled up to the school, it was like nothing she'd ever seen before: five enormous white igloo-like domes connected by hallways—but with no windows. She was hired immediately with a promise that she would be given her own classroom within two years. However, she would begin as a paraprofessional, helping Mrs. Carolyn Sween with her third grade class.

Martin was occupied with his police work and Lacy was finally living her dream of teaching. How could they know that a heinous presence, disguised as friendship, was going to disrupt their idyllic existence?

Martin's first weeks with Normal included in-house training to improve his proficiency in the skills required of a police officer. After the training, Martin was assigned to a car with a training officer. He wondered what his first official day in the field would be like.

Police work involves people, which means it's unpredictable. It also involves preventing those people from hurting each other—or themselves.

On his first day, a call came over the radio. "Station to fifty-six (Martin's badge number). We have a bike in the pond near the bridge."

"Fifty-six, copy," Martin replied into the radio. "We're on our way."

He drove to the pond and fished the bike out of the water with a special snaring device. Then they filled out the paperwork that is such a part of every cop's life. Martin was glad it had been a small event so he could take his time to familiarize himself with the various forms. It was the most tedious part of the job, but it had to be done in every case. Over time, Martin learned that no officer in Normal had ever shot anyone. Real police work was a lot different than TV cop shows. He knew he was going to excel at being a policeman.

Normal was divided into three sectors for policing purposes. One officer worked each sector and those officers worked under a lieutenant. Martin worked all three sectors at first. He needed to understand the city and how the department worked if he was going to be an efficient police officer.

After he'd worked all three sectors on the day shift, he was transferred to the afternoon shift. It was like a completely different job because the workload changed. It started after the kids were out of school and people were heading home from work. Misbehaving kids were chased, rush hour fender benders were written up, and traffic violators were cited. Martin sometimes wondered how he'd react to the first threat of violence or during a high speed chase—but he also knew that things like that rarely happened in Normal.

The people cops served and protected fell into four categories. The first were the whining victims who wanted some juvenile prankster hauled off to the electric chair because they had stolen the pink flamingo from their front yard.

The second category included genuine bad guys who made victims out of other people.

The third group was filled with drunks and stoners. Other officers would warn Martin, "He's not a bad guy when he's sober, but he's rarely sober. He'll sucker punch you first chance he gets, so watch yourself."

One afternoon, Martin was talking to his training officer, Ron, in the lobby of the station when an inebriated man walked in and said, "I'm fucked up, guys. Lock me up. I need a place to crash."

Ron shook his head and replied, pointing at Martin, "I can't do that, but if you were to punch this guy in the nose, I'd have to throw you in jail."

To Martin's relief, the drunk decided it wasn't worth having an assault-and-battery arrest on his record and stumbled back out the door. Ron and Martin shared a good laugh, which Martin found was a big part of police work.

The last people that cops had to protect were those who hung out with Mrs. Mental Illness—and they each challenged officers in their own special way.

Three sectors, three shifts, and four types of people. It was all slowly coming into focus, but it would be a lifetime learning process—but some lessons were going to be painful.

His last training took place on the night shift, when people started hanging around with Mr. Intoxication. Martin's greatest strength was his ability to understand things that could only be learned in the school of hard knocks. That was what had drawn Martin to police work in the first place.

New cops weren't allowed to argue with the older ones. They were expected to do what they were told until they made the grade—and you could only do that by encountering problems and working through them. College degrees meant nothing. Trust and respect only came from experience.

One wintry evening, Martin was called to his first domestic situation. When they arrived, he was instructed to kick the door in by the senior officer who had ridden with him. Martin had never done such a thing, so he relied on what he'd seen TV cops do—he planted his right foot on the top step and kicked the door with his left foot.

To his surprise, the door failed to give way, and the force of his kick sent Martin reeling backward—right into a snowdrift. As the senior officer tried not to laugh, Martin scrambled to his feet, climbed back onto the steps, and kicked the door again—this time while holding on to the railing.

The door still refused to slam open, but Martin's boot *did* go straight through, leaving him trapped and unable to move—not a good situation if a person on the other side of the door meant to do him harm. To add insult to injury, there was laughter from inside the house. Then the door opened and it took both the husband and wife to extricate Martin's leg from their front door.

After they drove away from the scene, Martin heard the senior officer say, "I guess maybe we need to add door kicking to our training regimen, huh, kid?"

That incident got Martin ribbed by the other officers for days afterward.

As his training continued, Martin discovered that there was more than one way to do a job correctly. Officers developed their own techniques for doing their jobs. Some loved filling out accident reports, some loved citing speeders, and others liked to deal with domestic disturbances.

Martin liked the parts of the job involving human interaction—and he especially liked to hold Mr. Intoxication accountable. He looked for the frightened eyes on the fringes of arrest scenes, watching Daddy being handcuffed and hauled off to jail. He always took the time to try to help them understand that Daddy would be coming home again, maybe better than ever.

However, some daddies didn't go to jail without a fight, and during those times, Martin would sometimes hear the daddy say something like, "Hey, let go of my balls!"

That meant Roger Max was the officer handling the situation. Max was skillful at wrestling a man into submission. He'd just reach for the crotch, grab, and squeeze. For some unknown reason, Max called his method "the Gleep," but whatever he called it, it worked beautifully. Max liked to say that when you had a man's balls in your hand, his heart and soul were nearby.

Mrs. Mental Illness was a constant companion of poor Mandy Honkings. The station received calls almost weekly and sometimes Mandy disappeared for several days. She lived in a little apartment on a busy street, and Mandy inevitably started hollering and setting up a commotion in the middle of the night, screaming about vampires or some other imagined threat to her life.

During one episode, when Martin arrived, he could see the genuine terror in Mandy's eyes, but besides disturbing the peace, she wasn't breaking any laws. He wouldn't arrest her—and she wouldn't have listened if he tried to explain that there were no such things as vampires.

He didn't know what to do, so he called his supervisor—Lieutenant Pullet.

After Martin had explained the situation, Badge said, "No problem, rookie. Put Mandy on the phone, will you?"

Once Mandy was listening, Badge said calmly, "Look, Mandy, you know we're here to help you, right?" As Mandy nodded, he continued, "I'm going to have Officer McMurphy sprinkle garlic around the apartment building. Vampires hate garlic, and they won't enter the building. Will that be okay with you?" When she said it would be acceptable, he then said, "Now can you give the phone back to Officer McMurphy?"

When Martin took the phone, Badge said, "I want you to go outside and start pretending like your sprinkling garlic powder all around the apartment building. Make it look convincing, because Mandy will be watching from her window. She needs to think you're surrounding the building with garlic powder to keep the vampires away."

"Right," Martin said, hanging up the phone. Then he turned to Mandy and said confidently, "I'll have the building completely surrounded with garlic powder in no time, ma'am. You can rest easy. You have my word that no vampires will ever bother this building again."

After she had walked Martin to the door, Mandy gave him a big hug to express her appreciation for his help.

He then gave an award-winning performance outside, pretending to cover the entire area with a liberal sprinkling of garlic powder. When he had finished, he looked up and gave Mandy a thumbs up. Badge had been right—she had been watching the whole time.

Back at the station, when Martin shared the vampire call with Justin Jones, one of the other officers, Justin said, "Well, get used to it. Now that you've taken care of her vampires, she'll dream up some other imaginary threat. Then all you'll have to do is figure out how to battle that new demon and she'll be satisfied."

While they were talking, Justin also gave Martin some candid advice. "Watch out for Badge. He only thinks of himself. If you screw up, it's on you, but if you do good, he'll take the credit. He's in it for himself—and as far as he's concerned, he's all that matters."

Martin was surprised by Justin's statement, but he agreed to watch his step around the lieutenant.

The night shift is polluted with sides of human nature the general public doesn't know exist. That was why police work was never boring for long. Martin's first year went by quickly, and although much of the work was routine, he was still learning new things almost daily.

One cool night, things were slow and no calls were coming in—until a domestic disturbance was reported on the west side. Neighbors had heard shouting and the breaking of glass, usually an indication that more than one officer would be required. Justin and Martin headed for the scene.

After knocking on the door and being told to go away, they entered the house and were confronted by a large wild-eyed man demanding that they show him a warrant. There were feathers stuck to the man's hand and floating around in the air. Martin saw a blood stain on the wall, and under the stain a dead cockatiel lay on the floor.

As Martin began looking around the room, Justin calmly tried to talk to the man, who was pointing at a cowering woman and demanding, "Get that sperm-belching bitch outta my life."

When it had become obvious that it was him the officers planned to arrest, the man switched tactics. He told them he had AIDS and would bite the first hand that was laid on him. It took some serious negotiation, but they finally were able to cart him off to jail. They also called an ambulance to take the poor battered woman to the hospital.

Later, Badge showed up at the ER as Martin was asking the woman questions for his report. The lieutenant always seemed to take his duties very seriously. However, as Martin scribbled in his notebook, he noticed that Badge had more on his mind than what was transpiring in the ER—and those thoughts seemed to involve the nurses he saw scurrying around doing their duties.

When Martin was finished, Badge stayed behind, seemingly intent on continuing to hit on the nurses. He was in the middle of telling several of them an involved story of his heroism and didn't even acknowledge Martin as he walked away.

Over the years, Martin tucked away a few stories of his own. A teenager dropped a bowling ball out of a twelve-story window and when it hit the sidewalk, it exploded, injuring people down below for a full block. Luckily for the teenager, none of them were hurt seriously.

Another time, a group of teenagers at the taco shop were chanting phrases like "no fetus can defeat us" and "we rape 'em, doctors scrape 'em" when a pair of pregnant women took offense and called the police. In a land of free speech, the teenagers hadn't committed a true crime, but that didn't make it any easier to mollify the tearful women.

It was a slow Sunday one night when Martin was sent out on a call concerning a depressed man who was marching around his house carrying a twelve-gauge shotgun. When he arrived, the man's wife pointed toward the front porch and pleaded, "He's over there. Please do something—quick!"

As Martin was warning the wife and children to get away from the house, he heard the shotgun go off with a huge blast that echoed through the neighborhood.

"You took too long to get here!" the wife screamed as Martin crept toward the front porch to see if the man had killed himself.

Maybe it was a trick, and the man was just waiting for him to show himself. Those were the kinds of mistakes that got officers killed.

Martin drew his gun and continued cautiously toward the porch, but he soon saw a terrible sight. The man had put the shotgun barrel into his mouth and pulled the trigger with his toe. The carnage was gruesome and Martin had to struggle mightily against the urge to vomit.

Looking up, he saw a sight that froze him in his tracks. The top of the man's head had been blasted onto the ceiling and was being held in place by brain matter and blood. As Martin looked up, his mouth agape in horror, a drop of the man's blood fell into his mouth. It was the most disgusting thing he had ever experienced. After the incident, Martin received a letter of commendation from the department, but it did nothing to erase the memory of that awful evening.

Police officers bring their job home at times when they've encountered something especially disturbing—and Martin was definitely disturbed by the suicide he had experienced that day. Lacy always took time to listen to what was on his mind. She also asked questions when something didn't make sense to her—things like how a suicidal man could reach the trigger on a shotgun while the barrel was in his mouth. Martin explained as much as he could about the incident, and was finally able to fall asleep, though the memory of another man's blood in his mouth wouldn't leave him any time soon.

Badge had also received a commendation for being the supervising officer that day, which didn't surprise the other officers. He had arrived after it was all over and consoled the grief-stricken widow, but he got to play the part of the knight in shining armor—something he was expert at and never missed an opportunity to do.

As the years went by, Martin enjoyed his time on the force. He had underestimated the community of Normal. There was always something going on, and he liked to be in the middle of the action.

The one thing he never quite adjusted to was the fact that there never seemed to be enough time to carefully consider the most prudent way of approaching a situation—and that meant he sometimes made mistakes.

Weekends meant parties and generally harmless fun—until things got out of control. On one autumn evening, a group of under-age adults conspired to get together and drink. There were always secluded spots to do that, and they picked a spot north of town, along the Root River. As they huddled around a campfire, one boy apparently got too comfortable with a girl who also had a boyfriend. The boyfriend stormed off, jumped into his car, stomped on the accelerator, and sped away.

As he approached a corner that couldn't be made at such a speed, his car flew off the road, bounced through a cornfield, and sailed across the river, ending up in a grove of willows. The call came in as a 10-52 personal injury accident for the single deputy, but when Martin heard it, he knew that such accidents sometimes turned into 10-54's, fatal accidents. He pointed his car toward the scene after getting clearance from Badge.

At the scene, the two officers grabbed medical equipment and ran across the field, only to encounter the icy river. There was ice at the edges of the waterline, and although wading through it would be necessary, it wasn't appealing.

A quick glance up and down the river revealed a 4x8 sheet of plywood that had gotten hung up in the river, and Martin suggested using it to cross the river. Being younger and more agile of the two, Martin said he would brave the crossing.

He stepped out with his left foot, but the plywood instantly gave way, sending Martin headfirst into the freezing water below. The other officer helped him out of the water, then crossed the river himself, where he discovered that the car had only been steaming, not smoking, and that the driver was banged up, but not dying.

As Martin headed for his patrol car, the other officer joked, "We had work to do, but you decided you wanted to go for a swim."

The kid was loaded into an ambulance shortly thereafter, and as Martin drove back toward Normal, he found himself thinking, "I suppose Badge will be headed for the kid's mom's house to comfort her—and to take all the bows."

When the chief decided to retire, he did everything in his power to make sure that Badge would be appointed to replace him. Badge was careful enough not to come right out and say it, but he wanted that job more than anything in the world.

The chief set it up so that Badge could attend the National Police Academy in Quantico, Virginia. Badge was delighted, but Agnes was distressed that she'd have to do her own grocery shopping. Badge busied himself looking through police supply catalogs so he could carry out the first change he would make once he became the chief. He would outfit the entire department with brand new badges—and his would be the biggest and gaudiest of them all.

The officers accepted the fact Badge would be the new chief. Justin told Martin, "The chief has been grooming old Badge for years. Nobody else has a snowballs chance in hell."

Badge had never been to any kind of leadership schools, and prior to joining the force, he had worked in a potato chip factory—but when the city posted the job description in the paper, as they were required to do, the first requirement listed was four years of Normal PD experience. Badge qualified in that regard. The second requirement was graduation from the National Academy. Badge was the only person on the force who also met that requirement—so he got the job.

To Martin's surprise, one of Badge's first official acts was to promote him—first to sergeant and then to deputy chief a short time later.

Badge discovered that promotions only changed outward appearances, and his life, devoid of any intimacy, made him resentful. In shopping malls or at church, he would gaze past his wife's enormous girth and long to have what other guys had on their arms—tits and ass! He wondered what it would be like to have a marriage that included sexual pleasures, and he cursed himself almost daily for not having the courage to have refused to say those dreadful words—*I do.*

It just wasn't fair. He was accomplished, virile, and consumed with passion. Sometimes he masturbated two or three times a day. He could never jeopardize his badge, but he needed a way to deal with the Urge, once and for all. What others possessed he longed to consume: their wives. He'd even gotten to the point where he offered prostitutes in the Twin Cities extra if they would wear a fake diamond wedding ring while he screwed them. He tipped them even more if they would moan that he was better than their husbands.

As police chief, Badge loved how special his fancy uniform and huge badge made him feel. Every time he put on his special dress uniform, he felt like an emperor from a bygone era.

Among themselves, the officers joked that maybe Badge would eventually want a diamond-encrusted crown, too. He began to pass out medals to officers for what seemed to be the most trivial things—to the point where they joked that they had to avoid the junkyard for fear of being sucked up by the gigantic magnet they used.

To be perfectly fair, Badge also contributed a few practical ideas, as well. He upgraded the squad cars and outfitted his officers with the latest crime-fighting equipment. After all, the Information Age had arrived in America, and Normal needed to be part of it.

But the Internet brought its own challenges for Badge. For years, he had managed to keep the Urge under control by taking personal care of sex calls whenever possible—but the Urge had been kept under wraps through masturbation and whores for too long.

Martin had continued to be careful with the comments he made around the department, even though he found it hard not to laugh when someone would say something like, "If I had a hog for a wife like Chief Pullet's, I'd pull it, too."

The only person he had felt safe confiding in was Lacy. She was his sounding board, his heart and soul, and his best source of advice. She was understanding and handled the duties of being married to a police officer with amazing grace and dignity.

She also proved to be an excellent teacher. She'd been working with fifth graders and enjoying all the challenges and rewards that came with being entrusted with the minds of young people. She was also happy when she and Martin began to talk about starting a family of their own and buying their first house.

Life was good and their future was bright—until Martin developed a big problem.

—Chapter 6—

Bye-Bye
"Hello, Goodbye" (The Beatles)

Sassy Beane had a sinister air about her. Anyone who crossed her path was aware of that in short order. When she was born, she was introduced to Mrs. Mental Illness by none other than Mr. Intoxication, and her father's drunken rages damaged her self-esteem beyond repair. Everything she did was wrong, and he never failed to let her know she was an ugly child in his eyes.

Her father would gaze at her, lowball in hand, and growl, "Christ, why couldn't you be born like other girls? You're nothing but bones and teeth—and now your mommy wants to put braces on them chompers. That'll set me back a pay check or two. God, I wish health insurance covered ugly daughters."

Using her babysitting money, Sassy tried makeup and expensive clothes, but nothing seemed to help. Her face and body were a prison she couldn't break out of. She'd pulled at her stringy hair and wonder why her boobs refused to grow—but one day they did, and she hoped deep inside that they would be her ticket to the happiness that had always eluded her.

The girls on the cheerleading squad laughed when they heard she wanted to try out—but try out, she did, even with her pale, pimply skin and a mouthful of braces.

As Sassy was doing her tryout routine, the captain of the squad leaned over to one of the other girls and said, "Look at her! She thinks she's something special just because she has the biggest tits in school. She's just a whore. Did you hear what she let the boys do after the football game last Friday night?"

Sometime during her freshman year, Sassy's much-anticipated breasts began to expand dramatically, and she quickly learned that boys would overlook pale skin and braces for an opportunity to paw at her. In her own contorted mind, Sassy Beane thought she was finally experiencing the love her father had always denied her.

Sassy also began to resent the other girls for their scorn. She was a good student and when she did well on a test, she loved to taunt the others. It was her only chance at a little payback, and she reveled in it. The more tears she could generate, the happier it made her.

When it came to her body, however, the other girls more than made up for Sassy's taunting remarks—and it was at its worst in the showers after gym class. She was always the last one in to avoid as much ridicule as possible. Nudity was far too uncomfortable, and the girls could be unbearably cruel.

As time went by, Sassy's frustration began to play with her mind. She started to become downright cruel—and she was determined to fight for what she wanted, no matter who got in her way. The other girls stopped making remarks—either in front of her or behind her back—for fear of retaliation. After amusing themselves with her voluptuous body, the boys discovered that their few moments of pleasure came at a heavy cost.

Ironically, even as she became a tyrant around her classmates, Sassy always went the extra mile for her teachers. She helped clean up after class and stayed after school if any of them asked for her help. She knew that authority and power was the key to success, and Sassy craved it as much as she craved the attention of a boy's probing fingers on weekend dates.

Sassy wanted power—something that had always eluded her. She equated power with safety and security—more than she had never known. If she was in charge, no one would dare point out her faults or be as cruel as her father had been. She craved the spotlight and longed for acceptance—if not adulation—and she was willing to do whatever it took to achieve that goal. Sassy just knew that somehow, someday, she would be important—and no obstacle or other human being would stand in her way.

Her college years weren't that much different from high school. She was self-centered and ruthless in the pursuit of her goals. If she was having difficulty in a class, she would wear a short skirt with no panties, sit in the front row, spread her legs—and improve her grade dramatically.

Sassy began to understand the awesome power of sex, and she used it as a potent weapon whenever it was necessary to get what she wanted. She was a player—and she knew the rules inside and out.

She could sleep with six or seven college boys and then lie back and taunt the ones who had come too fast. She delighted in the control sex gave her—power she had longed for all her life. The shame and humiliation she could dish out sent waves of pleasure into her very soul.

The day her father fell to the floor at work clutching his chest and struggling for breath should have been a tragic day for his daughter, but she actually rejoiced. No longer would that rotten bastard be able to hurt her with his slurred epithets. As far as Sassy was concerned, he could go straight to hell. It only seemed fair, since he'd made her life a hell on earth as long as she'd known him.

The death of her father felt like a triumph, but Sassy knew she was at the marrying age, which meant trying to find a guy who was actually worth keeping around. Life could be so unfair.

She finally snared a man she deemed to be a suitable mate—a slow-witted, spineless man named Junior. He was dull and stupid, but steady—and had somehow thought he had managed to knock her up.

For his part, Junior was touched by the knowledge that he had impregnated his girlfriend (which wasn't the case, but she never let him think differently). She was his girl after all—and though he wasn't the brightest crayon in the box, he did love Sassy with all his heart. As graduation approached, Sassy informed him that they were going to get married—and Junior happily agreed to the idea.

Junior soon said, "I do" and they lived happily ever after—until they left the church.

As time went by, Junior endured Sassy's sarcasm and cruelty with a gentle smile and a promise to do better. She was the aggressor, he was the fall guy, and they seemed made for each other, even if their marital arrangement made people who knew them uncomfortable.

Sassy would slip away at times to either service or be serviced by another man, according to her own peculiar whims. Junior was apparently the only person on earth who didn't know what was going on. He was pleasant, obedient, and clueless—three things Sassy appreciated in a spouse.

As slow as he might have been, Junior actually had a promising future with a large company, Wilson's. Soon he was bringing down a six-figure income, and the money helped Sassy immensely in her pursuit of power and recognition.

Junior never batted an eye when Sassy bore a healthy son—who didn't resemble him in the least. For her part, Sassy was just glad the child wasn't black, since she wasn't exactly sure who the father really was. Her life was moving forward exactly as she'd hoped. She had a meek husband who was nothing like her abusive father, she had lots of money, and she was finally in a position to start making people pay for all the pain and heartache she had endured as a child—and pay, they *would*.

Sassy obtained a position in the public school system after she and Junior moved to Normal. She wanted to rule a classroom, where she could decide who was worthy and who wasn't. However, before long, she grew restless. The principal was the real boss, and she decided that she didn't want to be stuck in a classroom with a bunch of sniffling brats. She wanted to run the school. She thought she was phenomenal and never hesitated to tell anyone just what she thought about herself. Sassy began ingratiating herself with the principal and taking classes to prepare herself for taking over the job, concealing her devious intentions behind a friendly smile.

Martin mastered the position of deputy chief quickly. He was young and eager, and he had Lacy by his side. She was also determined to be the best teacher she could be. Life was good, and they were enjoying it together as they both began pursuing master's degrees.

Once Sassy set her sights on becoming a principal, she set about undermining other principals at the various schools in the Normal district. After all, she couldn't get promoted if there were no vacancies. She searched for flaws—and then exploited them to insure maximum damage.

She'd say things like, "I don't want to cause any internal strife, but I feel that just this once I might have to be a tattler."

Then she would giggle as if she was uncomfortable—using the acting skills she'd perfected as a way to survive over the course of her unhappy life. She managed to sound concerned as she told a story based on the smallest nugget of truth to the superintendent, who listened graciously and sympathetically.

In an amazingly short time, Sassy became a principal in one of the district's smaller schools, but it was just the start, and she knew it. She immediately set her sights on the high school, and then on her ultimate goal—district superintendant. However, she'd first have to obtain a doctorate degree. People in the school system began to mumble about Sassy's meteoric rise—and began to avoid her whenever possible for fear of being the target of her wrath and manipulation.

In just a few years, Sassy was named superintendant of the Normal school system, but she couldn't shake the taunting voice of her father, telling her she was ugly and would never amount to anything. It made her more determined than ever to increase her power. She was radiant and smiling on the outside, but ruthless and determined on the inside.

Deputy Chief Martin McMurphy considered himself fortunate to be working in a department he loved. He had a genuine interest in people and excelled at helping them during difficult times. It was his life's calling, and it gave him immense satisfaction. He believed wholeheartedly in the justice system, and that drove him to want to accomplish even more.

One day, a neighbor, Matt Weinzeirl, called to Martin as he was bounding up the steps of his house. "Hey, Martin, do you think you could give me a hand with this?"

Matt had injured his back a few years earlier and was struggling to pull his garbage can out to the curb. "No problem, Matt," Martin said cheerfully. "You gotta watch that back!"

Sassy ruled over her school district with ruthless determination. She hovered over employees, and no one was safe from her steely gaze. If

Sassy wanted to promote somebody to an already-filled position, she used any means at her disposal to vacate that position. She threatened, she hounded, and she made people so miserable that they quit. It was that easy, and she felt no remorse. The reins of authority intoxicated her—even as the morale of the district began to slide.

Sassy was well aware that she needed to ingratiate herself to the people in power within the community. She sought out and spent time with the pillars of Normal. She was admitted to the Rotary Club, the Country Club, the Chamber of Commerce, and became a board member at the YMCA. She fawned over community leaders, doing whatever it took to appear to be everything she wasn't.

When she walked into the office of the chief of police, she immediately sized up Chief Pullet for what he was—exactly like her husband, a spineless wonder. His beady brown eyes, broad lipless smile, and outdated haircut were dead giveaways. She instantly knew he was a complete charlatan, and that knowledge would give her all the power over him she would need to accomplish her future goals.

"Welcome," Badge said, barely able to keep his leering eyes off Sassy's enormous breasts. "Please come in. I'm Chief Pullet, but you can call me Badge."

Smiling her most ingratiating smile, Sassy replied, instantly setting the ground rules for any future encounters, "Thank you, Chief Pullet. You may address me as Superintendent."

Then she went on, telling Badge exactly what she needed from him—and leaning over just enough to give him tantalizing views of her considerable cleavage. He was being lured into a trap from which there could be no escape, and the poor bastard didn't have the slightest clue.

"I stopped in to arrange for a brief meeting with you in my office regarding school security. Would that be possible, Chief Pullet?" Sassy asked, knowing full well that by that time Badge would have done anything she asked. "I'm all about the kids. We just have to keep them safe, and I'm hoping you'll help me make that possible."

She leaned forward again to emphasize her point as Badge sat mesmerized, nodding dumbly. "Yes, yes," Badge stammered. "Absolutely. I'm at your beck and call. Don't you worry. Badge is here!"

He was hers. Anything she wanted, he would do. It was all so easy.

Over the next few months, Sassy discovered something else she appreciated about Badge. He had an enormous penis and he loved to pleasure himself between a woman's legs. She played along with his perverted fantasies, letting him suck on her ring finger as he pounded her relentlessly, but she also had to admit that she enjoyed his rough lovemaking as he drove into her slippery body.

When she gasped, "Oh, Chief Pullet, I'm just a dirty little slut, cheating on my baby's daddy," Badge would climax forcefully.

She drained him of semen as efficiently as a milking machine sucks a Holstein dry—and took enormous pleasure in knowing that she had snared a police chief who couldn't refuse her tempting treats.

During Sassy's tenure as superintendent, morale among the school district's employees hit an all-time low. Teachers, paraprofessionals, cooks, bus drivers, and even custodians longed for relief. Their workplace was no longer a nice place to be. It had been contaminated by fear and intimidation. Something had to be done, but no one yet knew what that something might be, so they waited—and suffered.

—CHAPTER 7—

LOSIN' IT
"Escape" (Rupert Holmes)

Lacy became aware of the awful state of affairs Sassy was forcing on innocent people. While attending conferences or training seminars, stories were shared about the holocaust taking place in the Normal school district—chilling tales about what had been done to whom—and it was all very disheartening.

Martin was finally approached and asked if he'd be willing to see if he could do anything to improve conditions in the school district. He enjoyed a certain status in Normal from his exposure in the media regarding police matters and it was rumored that he might be electable. He was also aware of education issues because Lacy was a teacher.

Lacy and Martin had made a commitment to their community and had a strong desire to help wherever they could. Martin wasn't sure how he could contribute, but he was determined to try. Neither of them could have guessed that Badge had parked his penis in the superintendent and was therefore under her control.

76

Sassy's thirst for authority seemed to be unquenchable, and she was very protective of her power base. One aspect of that base was the Normal school board. However, it wasn't long before she made an unpleasant discovery. She learned that a man named Martin McMurphy had decided to run for a position on the board. It irritated her to realize that someone would have the audacity to run for such a position without her prior approval.

Untruthful people generally regard everyone as being just as devious as they are. The real cost of duplicitous behavior is a complete loss of trust in all other human beings, so Sassy immediately assumed the worst possible motives for Martin's desire to be on the school board. It was an unexpected challenge to her supremacy, and she launched an immediate investigation into what Martin McMurphy was all about.

"I don't like it," she snarled as she sat in her office one morning. "How can that guy think he can run for the school board without asking me first? It was probably those damn custodians who put him up to it. Well, I just might have a surprise for McMurphy and his janitor buddies."

Sassy trusted no one—and she certainly didn't trust McMurphy. She had worked too hard to get to where she was, and no one was going to mess with her. McMurphy obviously didn't know his place, and it was time to set that situation right.

Tapping her fingers on her desk, she thought, "I gotta know how to handle this clown. I already drilled the damn chief into his place. Maybe if I got McMurphy into my office I could screw some sense into him."

Sassy soon discovered that Martin wouldn't respond immediately to her phone calls, which infuriated her even more. She wasn't used to being ignored. Sassy seethed with hatred—which was further increased when the unthinkable happened.

Martin McMurphy won a seat on the school board.

The more Sassy thought about it, the more she began to associate

Martin McMurphy with everything that went wrong in her kingdom. He may have won the seat, but she had the chief of police by the balls— and Badge was Martin McMurphy's boss.

"Why haven't you called McMurphy off?" Sassy snarled at Badge after she had summoned him to her office.

Badge could only stammer, "I don't see what McMurphy—"

"Shut up!" Sassy snarled, silencing a thoroughly intimidated Badge. "I'll decide what McMurphy does or doesn't do, understand?"

"But—"

"I said shut up! You either do something about McMurphy or I'll make sure your so-called spotless legacy around here is gone forever— do you hear me? Call him off or you're finished. Am I making myself clear? Now get outta here!"

As Badge tried to think of something to say, Sassy dismissed him with a wave of her hand. He slunk out of her office, but as he walked down the hallway, his fear turned into anger. His days of steamy sex with sultry Sassy were numbered if he didn't do something about Martin right away—but what?

Then his thoughts turned to Sassy's threat to ruin his legacy. How could she do that without taking herself down at the same time? She wanted sex as badly as he did. As he thought, his anger turned back into fear. He had always played it safe when it came to satisfying the Urge until Sassy got a hold of him.

Then his fear turned into panic. Of all the people in the world, he knew Sassy was capable of carrying out her threat. He'd never been under attack like that before. Sassy was one scary wench, and she wasn't the type to bluff. He had no choice. Martin McMurphy would have to be dealt with—and soon.

His panic then morphed back to anger. No fresh kid was going to waltz in and destroy what had taken him a lifetime to build. He was the chief, and he'd find a way to bring Martin McMurphy down somehow.

When a computer first arrived in Badge's office, it gave him nothing but grief. He had to take classes to learn how to use it—and then it always seemed to be crashing. It was fear and loathing at first sight, but it would turn to love before long. Soon after he turned it on, it began to turn him on in return—when he discovered the Internet.

While working as a policeman, Badge had mostly managed to keep the Urge under control, but with the advent of the World Wide Web, the Urge refused to take a backseat. Sex, feelings of entitlement, and anonymity, all meshed together to allow the Urge to start occupying an ever-increasing amount of time. Badge could take chances on the Internet that he never would have considered in reality.

Over time, he came to regard his computer as a carnival of carnal delights. The Urge had escaped his control and muscled its way to the forefront. At first Badge treated himself to an occasional dirty little peek, but it didn't take long before those peeks turned into minutes, which then turned into wonderful hours of staring at naked women having sex—and he was especially attracted to videos of women who were cheating on their husbands.

Feeding the Urge made him rock hard and got even stronger as the weeks passed. Badge would lock himself in his office, accompanied by the Urge, and explore the never-ending wonder of watching wives having sex with strangers. His sexually charged state of mind would quickly drive him toward a finish, but he always came back for more.

Casual looking led to emails, which then led to picture swapping. It wasn't as if he was really hurting anybody. They were all adults, just having a little fun. He wasn't really being derelict in his duty. It was when the picture exchanges led to phone calls that Badge began to lose sight of his original passion and push the envelope.

"Oh, baby, do you play in person?"

"I'd love to, but how can we hook up? Nobody can know!"

"I know all about being discreet, sweetheart. I'm married, too, don't forget."

He had finally done it—arranged for a real meet-up with a married woman who would give the Urge what it had been craving for *free*.

Everything went just as he had planned during his first in-person sexual escapade. The woman had told him she wanted no drama—just sex. With that understanding, they went after each other like honey badgers in heat, then went their separate ways. It was easy and sleazy—and the best part was that no money exchanged hands.

After this first skin encounter, alone time with just his hands and dirty thoughts would never do. He needed real sex. He started checking his emails first thing in the morning for women who wanted to talk dirty to him. The Urge was so excited with the Internet that eventually the workday just didn't seem long enough. Fed by images on the screen and dirty words on the phone, the Urge sent orgasmic jolts of pleasure to Badge's brain—pushing his first love—his badge—further and further from his thoughts.

If a woman's husband didn't understand her, Badge found out what she needed, then gave it to her—and she did the same for him. She'd get wide-eyed as his pants hit the floor and would spend a wonderful night wrestling with his trouser python, but once it was over, Badge lost interest. Once he had defiled her, the thrill was gone. He'd move on to another man's bride.

Even while pursuing his perverse passion, Badge maintained his aura of perfection, although his badge didn't get shined nearly as much. He was known on the Internet as "The Blue Veiner Bride Pleaser." He loved oral and all sexual positions. It was easy to hook up with wives, and they felt safe with him. They could see him on the Normal website, smiling for the camera: Police Chief Charles Pullet.

He'd had many encounters before he finally screwed up. He was a good listener and always knew when Agnes had to be at the capital. When she was gone, he actually bedded married women in his own house. After Agnes was told that he couldn't get off work, her parents would arrive to run her up to the capital and he was free to play to his heart's content. Agnes never suspected a thing.

He snapped a photo of his erect penis and posted it next to his Internet moniker, The Blue Veiner Bride Pleaser. A short time later, a woman from Alaska emailed him saying that if he was "up" for the challenge she would try to "cum" to Minnesota. She and her husband ran a salmon business and she traveled to Motley, Minnesota, several times a year, she said. She got along with her husband but had always wondered how it would feel to be with such a big fella. She also sent pictures of herself in a black garter and nylons that made him gasp with lust.

When they talked by phone, she asked, "Baby, are you really as big as advertised? I'll be upset if you're playing games. I want no-strings-attached sex. Are you on board, or should I say on *broad*?"

"Baby, I'm gonna make you purr," Badge replied. "I'm even bigger in person and I'll keep it up until you beg me to cum. Are you gonna be a good little girl and wear your nylons for me?"

She told him that she'd be playing with a huge dildo so she'd be ready for him when they got together. She said a girl would have to be stretched a tad to accommodate his immense package.

After that initial conversation, they talked daily to keep the lust building.

Badge had become reckless, and even though he knew there was a chance that the city would find out about his lascivious behavior, the Urge wouldn't let him stop. All he could think about was the day he would finally get to meet up with the mysterious woman from Alaska.

Mrs. Alaska even told him a secret. She got turned on when a man growled in a low, mean voice, like a grizzly bear. On the phone, Badge practiced his growling while she spurred him on with her moans. She said his growling made her cum, and her moaning, coupled with his right hand, made him cum. He had always wanted to please a woman like Mrs. Alaska, and he was doing it!

Mrs. Alaska lived in Fairbanks and wasn't coming to Minnesota for a while, but she'd gotten Badge so turned on that he started trading pictures with girls who lived closer to Normal to help satisfy the Urge in the meantime—but no women from Normal. After all, adulterous sex was something Mother would never have approved of and Agnes could never know, either.

Badge had finally created the lifestyle he had always dreamed of. Women loved hooking up with him, since he was a cop and could be trusted. After sex they'd become strangers again because nobody could ever know.

A lady friend would occasionally request that he "glove up," though Badge preferred bare-backing and leaving his conquests lying in wet spots of contempt.

"No glove, no love," she'd say. "Please slap this on."

It didn't take Badge long to set her straight. "I've never been with another woman and I don't sleep with my wife. She doesn't understand me, no way, no how. I don't want anything to come between us, so you'll just have to trust me."

The woman would say, "You're not mad, are you? Take me. I believe you. Please take me. You're so huge."

Before he was done, the woman would end up panting with gratitude and taking his sperm without protection.

Sometimes Badge also worried about being out of control, like an alcoholic who wonders how it could have gotten to such a point. He knew he was being careless, but he was in denial and lost in his lies. Any concerns about getting caught were soon washed away by powerful waves of semen.

Badge loved disciplining officers when he thought they needed it—which meant any time he thought their actions might make him look bad in the eyes of the public. If cops were dumb enough to get caught, it was his responsibility to discipline them—and he disciplined officers for offenses far less grievous than the things he was doing. For instance, several officers had passed around an adult video tape which was going to be played at a bachelor party. When this was pointed out to Badge, he reprimanded the officers firmly.

He had spent an entire lifetime lying to himself to make things right in his head. He lied to his wife to make her life easier. He lied to his mother so she could look upon him with undisturbed, loving eyes. With those excuses firmly implanted in his brain, his lying never bothered him. He was getting laid without using rubbers, lots of people respected him, and his life was idyllic—all because he lied so well. He felt safe in the zone of lies that had become his life.

The city manager did what Badge ordered, the city attorney answered to him, and the mayor was his personal friend. If he wanted to masturbate in his office, he would. If he wanted to bed married woman, he would. He had forgotten what it was like to be a mere mortal. The badge on his shirt made him truly believe that he was infallible—and that belief would lead to big problems.

Badge continued to embrace his lifestyle with reckless abandon. Ladies seemed to enjoy everything about him and they'd buy anything he told them. He stopped making promises to himself about quitting. It was impossible. All he lived for was his next opportunity to defile the sluts who came into his life via the Internet. Like flood water that rises until the dike is breached, Badge's lust would swell until it burst out of his body. He rushed into women's lives and then disappeared after he took what he wanted, leaving them in a sticky puddle of nothingness.

He continued to send out pictures of himself and would receive pictures of his intended targets in return. Sex had become an obsession. He couldn't get enough of the wives of unsuspecting husbands.

Badge caught the attention of women by wearing his uniform with the oversized badge while displaying his hard-on. Life was good and only seemed to get better with each passing day. He loved lying and making women squeal with pleasure. Other guys had always gotten what he wanted, but he was finally evening the score by banging their cheating wives and treating them like the sluts they really were.

However, there was still the problem of Sassy and Martin McMurphy, and he had no idea how to resolve it—but that would have to wait. Mrs. Alaska was finally coming to town.

Badge's sexual excitement threatened to overwhelm him—until Agnes called and asked him to drive her to the town of Madelia. He tried to tell her that he had to attend an important convention—which was a cover story for a meet-up with a redhead in Winona who was meant to be the warm-up act for Mrs. Alaska—but Agnes would have none of it.

—CHAPTER 8—

DANGEROUS LIAISONS
"One Way or Another" (Blondie)

Somebody in Madelia had some pictures of the capital. Agnes's life was small and isolated. All she had was her state capital—and pizza. Badge knew he wasn't going to get laid in Winona. The sow needed him to drive her to Madelia. The redhead would have to wait, but he'd get to her before too long.

When he got home from work, she was there—Agnes, the fantasy killer. He could never understand why everything about the capital was so important—but he had never allowed Agnes to grow. She'd been swallowed up by her loneliness, and Badge had kept it that way.

She had secret longings to be treated with love and respect, and her miserable life caused her to strike out in anger at times. She loved chocolate cake and often ate herself into a state of serenity. Agnes missed the unconditional love of her mother, and the only way she could recapture that feeling was to eat. It was unhealthy, but all she and the man she called her husband seemed to have in common was eating pizza together several times a week.

Long ago, she had told Badge about a couple who had glass pictures of some sort that she just had to see. She made it sound as if they had hit it off right away, though it wasn't true. In fact, she had found their behavior revolting, but she told Badge they were a nice young couple. She'd gotten their names but had been in such a hurry to get to Badge's promotional party that she'd lost the slip of paper—and she had always blamed Badge for that.

"It was your fault, you know that," she said one day. "I could have contributed to the capital's legacy, but you caused me to lose the information, and I'll never forgive you for that. But now, as luck would have it, the young lady called me! It was lucky I gave her my number—and that she isn't married to someone as self-centered as you. You have to escort me to Madelia. It's that simple."

"All right," Badge conceded. "Let's go."

So instead of a steamy date with the redhead, Badge was getting the car ready for the drive to Madelia. He told Agnes he had to go to the office to clean up some unfinished business first, but he really needed some intimate time with his computer. He also had to call the redhead and cancel their date.

At the office, he found thirteen messages from Sassy on his answering machine. Was he going to call Martin off or not? He was getting under her skin and it *had* to stop!

Although he hated admitting his mistakes, Badge knew that when Sassy had enticed him to mount her, he had made a monumental mistake. He simply had to find a way get that woman out of his world. He vowed to do something about Martin—and Sassy—as soon as he returned from Agnes's road trip.

When they arrived in Madelia, the address was easy to find. Badge knocked on the door while Agnes stayed in the car. When the door opened, Badge was startled to be standing in the presence of an overwhelming beauty. She had deep blue eyes and long raven-black hair that fell to her shoulders. She was young and smiling her brightest smile. The Urge instantly snapped to attention. He had to try to park his cock in that bird.

His mind racing, Badge managed to stammer, "Good afternoon. My name is Charles Pullet, but you can call me Badge. I'm chief of police in Normal. I believe you had a discussion with the lady in the car regarding some pictures of the state capital."

"Yes," the woman said. "I'm Robin Johnson. Please come in."

"Thank you. I'm helping the lady in the car, who is curator at the capital. She seems to think that your pictures could be valuable, so the governor asked if I could help," Badge said, wondering if the woman could tell that he was telling her a load of lies.

For her part, Robin was surprised that the pictures were being treated as such important documents—important enough to send a chief of police and a curator to examine them.

"Well, if you'll go get the lady in the car, I'll show you the pictures," said Robin.

Badge was uncomfortable about assisting Agnes out of the car and then up to the house. He didn't want her shooting her mouth off and ruining his chances with this raving beauty. As he was helping Agnes into the house, a thought of Sassy suddenly sprang into his thoughts, but he rudely shoved it out of his mind. He wanted to concentrate on the lovely Robin—and how to get her to buy what he was selling.

While Agnes was eagerly looking at the glass plates, Badge did everything in his power to underscore his interest in Robin. He knew she'd be the star of his masturbation sessions from that moment on. She was his ideal woman and he wanted to fulfill his desires at the altar of her loins. Agnes was so preoccupied by the objects in her hands that Badge could have been making love to Robin on the couch next to her at that moment and she wouldn't have noticed.

The plates were in perfect condition and showed scenes of the capital building under construction. Agnes couldn't believe what she was seeing. They were simply amazing. After Agnes said that she was sure the governor would like to see them, Robin explained that her husband was a long-haul truck driver and she worked at a local nursing home. She then said that times were tight and that they'd be interested in selling them.

Then she added, "Oh, I have to introduce you to Peachy, my African Grey parrot. He can talk and make all kinds of noises."

When they walked toward the cage, Badge followed behind, mesmerized by Robin's perfectly shaped ass. He was obsessed with the possibility of getting to know it much more intimately in the future.

As they said their goodbyes at the door, Badge said effusively, "Your bird is amazing. Thank you so much. I hope to get to see you again soon."

Robin was forthright in her response, as well. "You're really the first policeman I've ever spent time with. You must be brave to do what you do. I've been a good girl all my life, so it's not like I've ever gotten a speeding ticket or been handcuffed."

As Robin giggled at her little double entendre, Badge was burning with lust in every cell of his body. He finally pulled himself away from her presence and joined Agnes in the car.

On the way home, he realized that he hadn't given Mrs. Alaska a thought after he had been introduced to ravishing Robin.

Agnes looked at him as they drove down the freeway and asked, "What's got into you? You've never cared about my work before."

Badge just smiled and lied, "I was glad I got to help you out, Agnes."

For once in her life, Agnes had done something good for him. Robin's husband was a truck driver—and he was a chief of police. There would be no comparison in Robin's mind once she fully understood his importance. She had it all—looks, a great ass, and a wedding band.

Badge had bedded some ugly women, which was okay if they were married, but Robin was a grand slam. He heard nothing of whatever Agnes was yammering on the way home. All he could think about was the dreamy look that would be on Robin's face as he entered her.

Robin was thrilled to think the glass pictures seemed to be worth something. Chimlyn had agreed to find out how much they were worth. They'd been stuck as renters for years and had never been able to save enough to buy a house. She had continued to hope that things would work out, but the store had closed and Chimlyn was gone all the time. It seemed as if even after he got home, there was only time for a shower and lots of sleep before he was on the road again. Robin hated being alone all the time. Truck diving wasn't working for her.

Robin had taken bookkeeping courses at South Central Technical College in North Mankato, but just as she completed her studies, the store closed. People in Madelia hated to see the store fold but it was their own fault for driving twenty-five miles to save a few pennies.

Chimlyn always seemed to be just a little behind, making long truck runs from places like Nevada to Chicago. Then when it came to pay day, he never seemed to get what he was supposed to. Robin was frustrated and went to work wearing a smile that masked her desire for something better in her life. She had never expected that she would end up working at the Madelia Nursing Home.

When she met the fat lady and police chief, she was intrigued. He seemed to be nice, funny, and friendly and was interested in her. Robin knew about cops from TV. They were the good guys, smart and brave, and always helping people. Robin had been taught to respect authority and had followed most of the rules while growing up. There had been times when she puffed on a cigarette and drank a wine cooler when the gang hung out at the Barn, but she had to do that to fit in with the crowd. She knew it was wrong to drink, though, and that she could have gotten jailed in Red Wing if she had been caught drinking.

Robin was thrilled to know that she had met an important man. He even worked with the governor. He'd asked her to call him Badge, so she must have made a favorable impression. It was fun to dream about being with an important man like Badge. It made her feel important, too.

It seemed as if life was passing her by. What else was there to do but dream? Maybe the glass plates would finally be the break she and Chimlyn had been hoping for.

While urinating before going to bed, Badge felt a burning sensation, like razor blades in his penis. He also discovered that whitish stuff was dripping out of his lady pleaser. Badge found himself going to the bathroom more—and it hurt like a bitch every time he did.

Badge cut out of work early one afternoon and went to the clinic. He hadn't told Agnes about his problem. He just told her he had a sore throat and not to worry.

But Agnes did worry. If she lost Badge, who would take care of her? Her parents weren't getting any younger and she hated the thought of having to do public things like buying groceries or getting the car fixed. Badge never wanted to see a doctor, so Agnes worried.

Badge stood with his mouth open, trying to comprehend what the doctor was telling him—a doctor from Normal who knew him. His mind seemed to have frozen and he was having a difficult time getting it started again.

"You've been infected with chlamydia and gonorrhea. I'm glad you came in. A shot of Ceftriaxone and another of Azithromycin should do the trick. We'll still carry out the confirmations with the necessary cultures. You notify your sexual partner about it, though. We need to treat anyone you've been intimate with. They may not even know they were infected, and it can get serious if it's not treated."

Badge's lying mouth finally sputtered to life. "I've been having marital problems. Agnes has been seeing someone in the Cities—someone she went to school with. I'll have to sit down and tell her to get treated, along with her boyfriend. I never thought it would come to this. I'm a married man. I know how harmful these diseases can be, so I'll address the issue, I promise."

The doctor was diplomatic and empathetic. He knew how painful a diagnosis of a sexually transmitted disease could be. "I must commend you for your actions, Badge," he said. "Sterility and kidney failure can occur if the situation is left untreated. Some women can even infect their unborn children."

Even as the doctor went on about his admiration and sympathy, Badge was deciding to let all the various women he'd infected find out on their own. He also wondered which one of them had infected him in the first place. When he was on the computer, flirting and having fun, he had never realized that the married gals he was screwing might have been banging other guys, too.

In the midst of all that, he also knew that he was going to call Robin the next morning. He wanted to taste her sexuality, and if she got infected in the process, that would be her problem.

In the office the next morning, Badge phoned his intended target before starting his regular police business. The conversation went smoothly and he could feel the Urge slithering around in his pants. It wanted out to be kissed and licked. Badge had to do something about it, and that something was called Robin.

"Robin? Badge here. I thought I'd call and let you know that the governor was impressed with your photographs. When can he meet you? I can pick you up."

"Well, should I wait for Chimlyn, my husband, so we can all go see the governor?" Robin asked excitedly.

"When does your husband get back to town?"

"Two weeks, I think, but that might change."

"I'm sorry, but it will have to be before that. We can't keep the governor waiting. I'll pick you up and we can have dinner on the way to the Cities. You pay enough taxes, so the state can buy you dinner!"

Robin couldn't believe her luck. She was going with a police chief to see the governor, and the state might want to buy the pictures. Also, Badge made her laugh and she'd be safe in the big city with a law enforcement officer. Robin forgot to ask if the big lady would be going along. She discussed her plans with her supervisor who had said it wouldn't be a problem to take a day off.

Badge told Agnes he was going to a convention for one night. He asked if she wanted to go along, knowing full well she would refuse. Agnes was as predictable as she was big, and she never seemed to suspect a thing.

Badge didn't plan to hurt Robin or anything, but she was a beauty and he had to have her. It would be like taking candy from a baby.

Badge still hadn't figured out how to get Sassy off his back. He wished Martin had never been promoted. Martin was always trying to change things. What did a cop know about schools anyway? It didn't make sense.

It also was worrisome that Martin had stumbled onto pictures Badge had taken of his penis next to the office copier. Badge also wondered what else Martin knew. Had he overheard phone conversations or wondered why Badge locked himself in his office for hours at a time?

Badge knew he couldn't duck Sassy forever—and when she finally did catch up to him, she was none too happy. "You think you're such a big honcho," she taunted. "Well, let me tell you this. I tried to make things work out, but you wouldn't help me."

"Now calm down, Sassy," Badge said. "I'll do something but—"

Sassy cut him off, letting him know in no uncertain terms that this was his last warning. If he didn't do something—and soon—she would expose him for the fraud he was, and he knew full well that she wasn't just talking. He didn't know why Sassy was so angry with Martin, but it didn't matter. He had to do *something* to save his career.

—CHAPTER 9—

TAKIN' ADVANTAGE
"Pretty Woman" (Roy Orbison)

The Pontiac Sunbird must have been breaking the sound barrier when the kid lost control on the black ice. After a whole lot of rolling, the kid was thrown from the car and tumbled at least a hundred yards across a frozen field. He ended up a bloody pile of goo with bluish white bones sticking out all over. Nobody could tell for sure what color the car had been. It had burst into flames and turned into a charred black hunk of steel before the accident was reported.

Officers raced across the furrows, and as the first officer turned the body over, he was staring into a death mask attached to a pulpy tangle of entrails. It was only after he dug a wallet out of the body that he recognized the kid. It was his backup officer's son—the same officer who was still struggling over the furrows with a medical bag and cussing out little bastards who drove like goddamn idiots.

"Christ, there are brains and shit scattered for sixty yards!" the second officer hollered as he drew closer.

There are times when police officers encounter issues during the performance of their duties that become personal—very personal.

Martin had struggled to help Matt because of his back problems. Lifting things for him and picking up his medication were the easy parts. The more difficult problems involved Matt's apparent misuse of his medication. Martin couldn't understand how a doctor would prescribe something that would cause Matt to be so out of it. At times they couldn't even go fishing because Matt would, for all appearances, be sleepwalking.

"Matt, you're not doing so good," Martin told him one day. "I'm serious. You look like shit. You've got to change medication or something. This stuff is making a zombie out of you."

"I'll be okay," Matt replied with a shrug. "I'm just having a bad day."

Lacy's life was going beautifully, as far as she was concerned. They had discussed having children now that their careers were well underway.

"You get to name the boys and I'll name the girls. That's fair, right?" she asked Martin.

"If it's a boy, we'll call him Dylan, after my favorite writer, Dylan Thomas," Martin replied. "Or how about Avis? That sounds okay, too."

"Anna and Ashley," Lacy said, having obviously been thinking of names already.

When the dead body call came in, Martin grimaced. He knew immediately that it had been Matt Weinzeirl. Not only had Matt lost his struggle with painkillers, but Martin had also lost a good neighbor and a friend.

It was later determined that the substance that had killed Matt was Oxycontin—the painkiller he'd been taking. Martin continued to ask questions, taking some of Matt's pills from a burn barrel, along with a variety of other items—former evidence, trash, and unclaimed stuff turned in to the Law Enforcement Center—back to his office to consider. If he could understand why Matt had died, perhaps he could help others avoid the same fate.

As Martin sat looking at the medication bottle, another officer walked in. Not wanting to have to explain the tangle of emotions he was feeling, Martin quickly stuffed the bottle into his pocket. However, the officer then reported what he had seen to Badge, telling the chief that Martin had acted suspiciously and might need help if he was abusing a potentially dangerous prescription drug.

"Chief," said the officer, "I saw McMurphy stuff what looked like a pill bottle into his pocket when I walked into the room. I just thought you should know."

Badge thanked the officer and then ushered him out of his office. As he sat back down behind his desk, he thought about something Sassy had said during their last conversation. She said McMurphy had been acting strangely. Now he had an officer telling him that McMurphy was acting suspicious. He smiled at the thought of it. He might finally have been given his golden opportunity to rid himself of McMurphy and get Sassy off his back.

Badge immediately called Martin into his office, after he had taken a chair in front of the chief's desk, Badge said, "Martin, you and I need to have a talk. You've been upsetting a lot of people in the community lately—school folks, other cops, and Superintendent Beane—and I'm afraid I've got to do something about it. You haven't been yourself lately, and I've been led to understand that you put a bottle of something in your pocket when another officer walked into your office. For the sake of the department, I have to ask you to tell me about that bottle—right now."

Martin smiled and said, "It's just a bottle of the painkiller that killed my friend, Matt. If you think I'm on drugs, Chief, I'll take a test to clear the air. If you come to my office, I'll show you the bottle. I locked it in my desk drawer."

Although the explanation made sense, Badge knew he couldn't let the opportunity slip away. If he could make everyone believe that Martin had developed a drug problem, it would solve everything. Sassy would be happy again, and Martin's credibility would be ruined, just in case he decided to tell whatever damning information he had obtained.

Badge didn't even bother to look at the evidence. He put Martin on an indefinite unpaid administrative leave. Martin got a strong feeling that he wasn't being told the entire story as he was unceremoniously being ushered out of the building.

When Badge called to let Sassy know that he had essentially dismissed McMurphy from the department, she snarled, "Yeah, right."

Her blasé response unnerved Badge. He had expected her to be ecstatic.

Just in case she hadn't understood, he reiterated, "McMurphy has been taken care of. He won't be causing you any more problems."

"Cut the shit, Badge," Sassy said sarcastically. "You don't have the balls to just get rid of him. You want to tell me what really happened?"

Badge sighed, then said, "Okay, but remember, this has to stay between—"

"Look, Badge. Give it to me straight and fast—and remember, you don't call the shots around here. I do. You got that?" Sassy interrupted.

In Sassy's eyes, Badge and Junior were like two peas in a pod, though she had to admit Badge had a bigger "pod." They were safe, stupid, good little boys who did whatever she told them to do—and it annoyed her when they refused to keep their traps shut!

Screwing and sucking to get what she wanted had always come naturally for Sassy. She liked the power rush she got when men bent to her will—but she detested guys with no balls—like that nutless Junior or that sniffling coward called Badge.

Badge was relieved when he finally got off the phone. Sassy hadn't taken the news anything like he thought she would. He hoped she had gotten a dose of the clap from him. It would serve her right. He was also glad he hadn't gone to her office to give her the news. She would have chewed him out even longer in person.

Agnes was upset when Badge showed up late for lunch at home. "I suppose something came up, huh?" she asked. "And I suppose you didn't think to call me and tell me you were going to be late?"

Sipping a cup of coffee, Badge tried to act cool and calm as he reminded Agnes that he was headed to Mankato for a convention later that afternoon and would be gone overnight.

"Why don't you drop whatever you're up to and come along?" Badge urged. "It'd be nice to spend some time together."

He knew Agnes hated venturing from the house into uncharted territory, but it never hurt to ask. It was the best way to keep her suspicions at bay.

After pausing a few moments, he asked again. "So what do you say? Would you like to go to Mankato with me?"

I can't go," Agnes replied almost apologetically. "You know how much my stomach hurts, so why do you even ask?"

Still playing the game, Badge asked, "Well, would you like me to pick you something up for your tummy?"

Badge smiled at his private thoughts. Nothing was going to rob him of the pleasure and anticipation he was feeling at that moment. He was closing in on the object of his desire, and it made anything bearable, even facing Agnes and Sassy on the same day. Robin was so young, pretty, and naive! It was almost going to be too easy.

"Do you need me to pick you up anything before I go?" he asked again.

Badge had coupled his untruthful nature with skills acquired from hustling chicks on the Internet, and he knew his chances with Robin were good. A cop was way better than a truck driver, and he was a chief!

"No, thanks," replied Agnes, obviously calming down. "Go enjoy yourself in Mankato, but if I'd have known how much you'd be out of town when you became chief, it would have never happened."

"Well, I do plan to enjoy myself in Mankato," Badge said—and he meant every word.

Badge was never happier than when he was headed out the door of that house—and away from Agnes. He had plans for a wonderful evening, beginning with a trip to the Westwood Marina on Lake Washington for dinner and drinks. It was an ideal place to set a romantic mood for the rest of the night.

Badge was so giddy that he didn't make love to his computer before hitting the road. He had never really bird-dogged an honest-to-goodness young girl before. He had only chased women on the Net, not counting Sassy and various whores.

Badge usually went after women close to his own age. As he headed toward his mission, Operation Young Sex, he glanced in the rearview mirror and saw that he had some grey streaks in his hair. He instantly changed his plans and headed to Walmart for some hair dye. He also picked up some cologne for use in the upcoming seduction game. The dyeing business was tricky. He had to comb it in and then rinse it out at a rest area on the west side of Normal. Even if it didn't actually knock off any years, it made him feel younger.

He was driving an unmarked car, complete with a police radio, to reassure Robin how important he was. When he arrived at Robin's place, she was charming and intoxicating as only a very young woman can be. He was beside himself with lust. He needed her until he could make her destroy her vows—and then he'd move on to his next conquest. The Urge had to be satisfied, and Robin would soon provide that satisfaction. He wanted to know how she'd taste and how her body would feel.

He loved the talking dirty thing and some of his bed partners would gasp and pant (at his coaxing, of course), "Give it to me, Badge! You're better than anyone who has ever put it to me." He always came when a woman was moaning his praises the loudest.

He found relief behind his huge badge. It was proof that he was an important man and it helped him get what he wanted. He had left the dragon behind, happily munching on pizza, and nothing was going to stand in the way of his conquest of Robin that night.

When Robin woke up that morning, she hadn't been able to decide what to wear. She had never met a governor before, and she was both excited and terrified.

The night before, while talking to Chimlyn on the phone, she hadn't told him about her plans. She wanted to surprise him, and if everything worked out the way she was hoping, he would be able to get off the road and stay with her where he belonged.

She put on her favorite bikini panties, which were white with fine pink stripes. She knew Governor Dayton would never see them, but she was trying to be thorough, even to the point of her favorite panties. She also put on black silky dress slacks and a matching blazer. Both the slacks and the blazer had fine grey matching stripes. It was her favorite ensemble. She finally settled on a sheer light grey shirt to finish off the outfit.

After brushing her lightly-permed hair, she drank a cup of coffee and nibbled on a piece of toast. She was too nervous to eat much, but she needed something in her stomach. She didn't want to be embarrassed by a grumbling tummy. She couldn't wait for the chief and the heavy lady to show up so they could begin their adventure.

Finally, she saw Badge pull up to the house and hop out of the car—but he was alone. She let Badge knock on the door before answering it, smiling and giggling nervously. Badge interpreted her behavior to mean that she was eager for their "date" to begin.

"Come in, please," Robin said. "Why isn't the other lady with you? I have the glass plates all wrapped up and ready to go."

Badge said, "I'm sorry. Agnes is ill, but the governor would still like to see your pictures. We'll slip them into the trunk to keep them safe, and then head for St. Paul."

"Okeydokey!" Robin said, though she instantly wished she hadn't.

The chief would think she was a country bumpkin. He wasn't wearing a wedding ring, so he was probably single—although there was a whitish line on his ring finger where a ring had been.

"Can I see your Parrot? Peachy was his name, wasn't it?" Badge said, knowing Robin would be pleased that he had remembered.

"Sure," Robin said, obviously impressed. "I'll introduce you properly."

After stopping to gas up at the Kwik Trip, they headed north out of Madelia toward Mankato on Highway 169. Although Badge seemed to be quite interested, Robin realized that he might just be making polite conversation as he explained that although the governor's schedule was constantly changing, he hoped they would be able to dine with him. Robin could hardly believe she was in the company of someone as important as Badge and on her way to dine with the governor. Most of the people Robin knew bad-mouthed Governor Mark Dayton simply because he was a politician, but that didn't matter to her at that moment.

As he drove, Badge joked, "I'll have to strip search you for weapons to keep the governor safe, but don't worry. I'm a professional." When Robin gasped, Badge quickly added, "I'm kidding, Robin." As she relaxed, he went on. "You're a beautiful girl, and your husband is a lucky man. I'm sure that the governor will enjoy your company as much as I am."

Robin blushed slightly, but she was thinking, "I'm liking this chief. He's funny and he seems to like me for what I am. He's so mature and important—yet he remembered Peachy's name."

"We should stop in Mankato so I can check on Mark's, I mean Governor Dayton's schedule," Badge said, knowing he was slowly closing the net around his prey. "I can't talk to him on a cell phone—security, you know. Do you mind waiting in the car?"

"Not at all," Robin replied as Badge pulled the car into the parking lot of Pagliai's pizza parlor.

Inside the restaurant, Badge stood near the front entrance where Robin could easily see him. He flashed his badge to the kid at the counter and told him he needed to use the phone immediately. He also made sure that Robin had seen him throwing his weight around. It would impress her even more.

While pretending to be talking to someone on the phone, he dropped words like *national security* to impress the kid, who was obviously eavesdropping. Then he thanked the boy and walked back outside to rejoin Robin.

"Look, Robin," he said apologetically, "the governor got called to a meeting. I'm not at liberty to say what it's about, but you'll hear about it on the news. That's the bad news. The good news is that I'm now able to take you out to dinner myself. There's a place over on Lake Washington I think you'll like. It's got a big fireplace, great ambiance, and excellent food. It's the least the citizens of our state can do for you. You're all dressed up, so we might as well do something special. What do you think?"

Robin was in no hurry to get back to Madelia, so it only took a moment for her to accept Badge's proposition. She felt as safe with him as she would have with her father. He was old—and a *cop*, after all. She was in the big leagues, about to have dinner with a friend of the governor.

At the marina, they walked out onto the deck, looking at boats while ducks paddled around noisily, demanding bread and cracker crumbs. It was enchanting. Robin had envisioned herself having dinner in a place like that many times before, but had never had the chance.

When Badge asked what kind of wine she preferred, she was completely at a loss, but Badge just smiled and took control, making Robin feel totally at ease as the night flew by.

After they'd finished their tenderloin steak topped with mushrooms, Badge ordered another bottle of red wine with a fancy French name. Robin had never drunk so much before and it was beginning to catch up to her as Badge poured another glass, reminding her that their goal was to enjoy themselves and that he was driving.

After leaving the restaurant, they fed the ducks as the sun set over the lake. It was all very magical, and it was all perfectly orchestrated by Badge. It was so easy. She would be his before the night was over—of that he had no more doubt.

On the way home, they stopped at the Country Pub near St. Peter for after-dinner drinks in the Garden Room, though Badge had to order because Robin was getting sleepy and giggly. He ordered a drink made with amaretto, and Robin seemed to enjoy it very much.

Robin was having the time of her life. She hadn't met the governor, but Badge had made the night something she knew she'd never forget. The other people in the Garden Room probably thought Robin was Badge's younger sister, but he didn't care. The time was approaching when he'd make his move.

As Badge helped the now thoroughly inebriated Robin out to the car, she was laughing and singing. It was obvious that she trusted him completely—which made him want her even more.

After driving a short distance, Badge suddenly pulled into a motel and said apologetically that he'd had more to drink than he should have and thought it would be sensible for them to make an unscheduled stop in the interest of safety. Through her alcoholic haze, all Robin really heard was Badge telling her that they were going to be forced to share a room because of a convention or something in town.

Once in the room, she passed out the instant her head hit the pillow—but she was awakened by Badge entering her. The booze helped, but it still hurt as he pushed into her. She was naked, but she didn't remember getting undressed. Things had gotten out of control, and something told her it was wrong.

As she felt the warmth of his semen on her inner thigh, she began to regain some of her senses. Why was she naked with this man? What would Chimlyn think of her if he ever found out?

After settling his first craving, Badge had entered her again. He came faster than usual—this time directing his semen onto her wedding ring. The entire night had been everything he had hoped for and more.

In the morning, Robin's stomach felt like it wasn't open for business. Badge was smug and controlled, but Robin was confused. He acted cool and somewhat apologetic, claiming that he didn't remember quite what had happened. He also told Robin that he had a wife and kids and didn't want anyone to get hurt due to the incident.

Robin would have been hurting more if she wasn't still numb from the entire experience. She had trusted Badge, but how could she forgive herself for letting something like that happen? He was a family man with a wife and kids, yet they both had somehow been unfaithful.

In her addled mental state, she began to believe it had somehow been her fault. She had gotten very drunk, after all, and she had been attracted to him. Maybe he simply hadn't been able to resist her advances.

Badge slyly told her that they needed to simply be honest with each other and admit that things had gotten out of hand. No one was at fault, he said, and if they simply accepted it as a one-time occurrence, no one would get hurt.

When they got back to Robin's house, Badge walked her to the door, but she suddenly felt as if she was going to vomit, so she dashed to the bathroom. That was fine with Badge. He lingered in the living room and stared into Peachy's yellow eyes. There was no way for him to know how bad it could get having Peachy out of his cage. He beat a hasty retreat out of the house without any awkward conversation about what had happened. He just got in the police car and headed for home—triumphant and satisfied.

Inside the house, Robin finished retching, she instantly began taking off her clothes so she could take a shower. She felt dirty and couldn't wait to wash away Badge's nastiness from the outside of her body—but the pain he had inflicted on the inside would take much longer to wash away.

—CHAPTER 10—

FINDING OUT
"Jealous Guy" (John Lennon)

Martin felt as if he was under attack from a thousand different ways. He loved the community of Normal and expected to have some of those feelings reciprocated. He had won a seat on the school board and truly wanted to do right by the district's employees.

Martin had also worked diligently for the police department and considered the people there more than mere colleagues. They were his friends, fellow officers, and first-rate guys. When he was put on administrative unpaid leave by Badge, both his life and his outlook were transformed. Times grew more difficult for Martin and Lacy.

Meanwhile, Badge wore the mask of a grieving, understanding friend and colleague. Martin agreed to meet with Badge or anyone else to clear up what he thought was a merely a misunderstanding. He also agreed to take a drug test.

During the meeting, Badge said matter-of-factly, "You'll need to meet with Superintendent Beane, so I'm ordering you to go to her office with me and beg for her forgiveness. She's expecting full transparency so she can put the incident behind her."

Although Martin was confused, he readily agreed to meet with Sassy, even though there was no apparent connection between his suspension and the superintendant of the school district.

"Sassy's good at running our school system," Badge said, "but of course you know that, since you're on the school board. She is all about the children, so we're going to march over there and you're going to give her what she wants. I expect you to be truthful and to treat Superintendent Beane with respect. If you don't she'll file a complaint and I'll have to take more stringent action. You'll make peace with her or I'll make your life miserable. Am I making myself perfectly clear?"

Badge knew full well that Sassy would be delighted with him for dragging Martin into her office—and he'd no longer have to worry about his legacy. He'd have Sassy off his ass and would be rid of Martin once and for all.

Badge believed that he was on the brink of some great things. He had laid a young thing in Madelia and then sent her scurrying back to her hubby. She had been sloppy drunk when he rode her, but she had wanted it. There was no doubt about that. He got to come on her ring, and he had kept her pink-striped panties as a souvenir, stored in the glove compartment of his squad car. It made him hard just thinking about them.

If he could keep Sassy and Agnes off his back, he could get back to more important things—like getting laid. Screwing intoxicated young things wasn't really his thing. She was pretty and all, but when she woke up, Robin hadn't acted like she wanted more. He preferred women off the Internet. They appreciated getting laid and liked talking dirty to him.

He was concerned that Agnes would want to see the pictures again, and he could only hope that Robin would be discreet and keep the whole episode to herself. Young girls sometimes had bigger mouths than his usual conquests.

"She's married, so she'll have to keep her trap shut," Badge tried to convince himself. "Things will work out okay. She believed me when I told her both of us were at fault."

Badge pulled up to his house and braced himself for what was to come. Agnes would be a black cloud, storming around the house. As he always did when she was like that, Badge knew it was best to take the path of least resistance. She'd be worked up about something, and he would simply nod as she raged on and on.

On the way home, Badge had played the Martin scenario over and over again in his mind until he finally began to believe that Martin really wasn't law enforcement material and would have to be run off. He simply couldn't tolerate having a cop on Oxycontin. The term *accountability* wasn't part of Badge's vocabulary, but it soon would be—covered with grey feathers.

When Badge finally entered the house, nobody was home. That had never happened before. Would she head to the Twin Cities without letting him know? She couldn't drive. It was all very strange.

"Agnes, are you home?" he called out as he strolled from room to room. "Where are you, dearest?"

Badge made a peanut butter and jelly sandwich and sat at the kitchen table, lost in his thoughts—and the feelings he was getting spooked him. It didn't make any sense at all.

Earlier, as she was waiting for Badge to come home for lunch, Agnes had received a phone call from a man who identified himself as David Dovekie.

Although he was obviously upset, Mr. Dovekie tried to be civil to Agnes. "Look, Mrs. Pullet, there's no easy way to put this. I'm calling to ask if you think you could keep your husband away from my wife. Can't he just leave us alone? We have kids!"

Mr. Dovekie went on to add that he loved his wife, in spite of what had happened, and he begged Agnes to promise him that she'd try to get her husband to quit bothering his Phoebe.

Agnes was stunned into silence by the call, and Mr. Dovekie seemed to understand, since it was clear that she'd had no knowledge of her husband's philandering. He explained that he and his wife were working things out, but he thought Agnes should know about the suffering her husband had caused. He was as kind as he could be under the circumstances, and before he hung up he promised to touch base with her again.

After she hung up the phone, Agnes sat at the kitchen table in a stupor, struggling to come to grips with the painful reality she had just learned about. Maybe Phoebe had been a husband stealer, intent on running away with Badge. But Mr. Dovekie had sounded so sincere that it didn't sound that way—which brought up a possibility that she just couldn't face.

She went to the bedroom and slid open the drawer where Badge kept his off-duty gun, a Smith and Wesson thirty-eight caliber revolver. She had seen Badge clean it often while watching TV. She had seen him repeatedly load it and unload it, a distant look on his face.

Her tears flowed copiously as she contemplated what she would do without Badge in her life. Without Badge, she would have no life.

She picked up the gun and slowly walked out to the garage. For some strange reason, she thought about something she'd heard on one of the afternoon talk shows, something about how women liked to kill themselves in ways that wouldn't mess their faces up. They wanted to look good, even in their caskets—but Agnes figured she'd put the bullet through the back of her head so it would blow her ugly, useless face off. No one had ever told her she was pretty, so she'd do the world a favor by not making anyone look at her face again. She could only hope that the damage would be so severe that the mortician wouldn't be able to repair her face. She imagined Badge lying to everyone, telling them that he had no idea why she would do something like that. That would be so typical of him.

Badge finished washing down his sandwich with a glass of milk, then realized that he hadn't checked the garage, although it wasn't a place Agnes ever spent any time, since she never drove. Still, a thorough good policeman would check the whole house, and Badge was a good policeman, so he stood and walked toward the garage door.

When he opened the door, he was stunned. Agnes was seated on a chair, holding the gun in her hands, apparently lost in thought. She didn't even flinch when he opened the door.

"Agnes!" Badge shouted. "For god's sake, what are you doing?"

For a moment, Agnes failed to respond. Then she turned her head toward him, her eyes full of hatred and disgust.

"How could you, you bastard?" she growled. "I try to do my best, and then you do something like this. Just leave me alone and go back to your whore—Phoebe. You've never been anything but a liar and a cheat, and I hate your guts, Mr. Perfect."

"Keep it down, Agnes!" Badge demanded. "Our neighbor is working on his trailer in the driveway next door. He'll think—"

"That's all you've ever cared about—what people think!" Agnes shouted. "What about me and what I think? Why have you started dyeing your hair? Does Phoebe like black hair?"

Although Badge was stunned, his cop mind took over and he began trying to calm Agnes down so he could at least get the gun out of her hands. He told her that he could explain everything, but even as he was talking, part of his brain was concerned that the neighbors would hear their argument. If Agnes put a hole in her head, it wouldn't look good for him—and the irony was that he hadn't even laid Mrs. Alaska yet. It just didn't seem fair somehow.

Badge put on a caring, concerned mask, using the same tone a trainer uses to calm down an unruly animal. "Agnes, we both know you can't judge a book by its cover. There's more to this than meets the eye, if you'll just let me explain."

He maneuvered the situation brilliantly, prodding Agnes into a conversation in the hope of discovering how much she knew. Then he could start constructing his lies to make it all go away. Didn't he have enough to worry about between Martin and Sassy? Now Agnes was complicating things even more. Life was so unfair. Why did things always happen to him?

As they talked, Agnes finally broke down, saying that she wanted to be a better person and a better wife—and Badge could tell that she really meant it, for the first time in her life. She asked if they could go to marriage counseling and Badge agreed, though it was only to take another step toward getting the gun away from her.

Finally she surrendered the gun and Badge reluctantly gave her a hug while she cried pitifully. Then he said cheerfully, "Look, Agnes, I'll go get some pizza. I'll be right back. Don't worry about a thing. We'll make it through this, I promise."

As Badge backed out of the driveway and drove toward the pizza shop, he wondered how Mrs. Alaska's husband had found out about them. He hated to lose her, but she was a threat to his perfect image. He decided to lay low and wait to hear from her.

Even so, he wasn't about to start giving up pussy just because Agnes was running around with his gun. He'd just have to be more careful.

As far as Phoebe went, he didn't quite know what to do. Her husband knew about them, but should he call and apologize? Badge was actually laughing as he stepped out of the car and headed into the pizzeria.

Then a strange thought hit him. If Agnes went to counseling, maybe she would find a new way of living. She definitely needed it—but he wouldn't go along. She was the one who needed fixing. He was the chief of police. He was perfect the way he was. Agnes was the one sitting in the garage with a gun pointed at her head.

The thought of it all made him angry. After all, he was a man, and he wouldn't let either his mother or Agnes make him out to be anything less than that. He'd show them! He'd have more sex with even more women. He wasn't a little boy anymore, and he was determined to screw his way into the safety of manhood. With patience, Agnes could be put back into her place, and he had the legal system to take care of Martin and to make Sassy happy. Some lying would also be in order, but that was no problem for Badge.

After Agnes had been dealt with, Badge continued his computer pleasures, back-filling the voids in his life with lusty adventures. He shoved all thoughts of the mystery husband out of his mind. Whenever he entered strange women, it was done with the protection of a condom, and he never rode the same woman twice—but in the back of his mind, Badge knew that Agnes was watching him.

He didn't recall pissing razor blades before Sassy took her pleasure from him. She only wanted the pleasures—no kissing or foreplay of any kind. After she had taken her pleasure and he had shot his own joy juice, they pulled their pants up and went about their business. It had all been unnatural, and it was coming back to haunt him.

Martin continued to hammer at Badge's peace of mind, and it irked Badge that Martin refused to go away. Badge called in investigators from outside the Normal police department to prove that Martin was a druggie, but Martin had passed the drug test with flying colors. The investigators also checked the entire police department, but could find nothing missing, yet Sassy had insisted that Martin had been acting strangely.

Badge knew that falsely accusing a fellow officer of a crime wouldn't be seen as an innocent mistake. It would make him look incompetent and less than perfect, and that was unacceptable.

Over time, Martin found himself drowning in a sea of injustice. Nothing was as he had believed it was. The justice system wasn't working, and the deck seemed to be stacked in favor of Badge and his lying ways. Badge had the entire system behind him—a city attorney at his beck and call, a city administrator who danced to whatever tune Badge played, and a mayor who was a personal friend.

Martin had refused to apologize to Sassy and had hired an attorney to challenge Badge in court. It was a big enough story that newspaper and television reporters set up camp in town.

When Robin started seeing Badge on the Mankato TV station, it brought back all the pain and suffering he had caused her. The more she revisited that evening, the more she realized that policemen weren't always heroes. Sometimes they were the villains. It galled her even more to see him on TV acting high and mighty and spouting lies.

Although she told no one, Robin saw Badge for the sinister person he really was. She stared at her tormentor on TV and felt her hatred and disgust grow like a cancer inside her. She remembered guys at the Barn making fun of girls who had found themselves in similar predicaments. She and her friends would yell at the boys to shut up, but they just laughed it off. It wasn't funny now, and she knew she'd have to do something about it sooner or later.

Badge had easily steered Agnes into a calmer state of mind by telling her he wanted to help with her problems. Together they found people on the Internet who were also having difficulties and commiserated with them, but they never met any of those people in real life.

Badge used that shared experience to his advantage, telling Agnes, "All I was doing was trying to help somebody out over the Internet, but I never met her in real life. We just chatted on the Internet, but her husband apparently read way too much into it. I'd never do anything to hurt your feelings, Agnes."

He then reassured her with a false smile and Agnes believed him—largely because she had no other options. Badge also played up the fact that the man had never gotten back to her like he had promised.

"How can you trust someone like that?" he asked. "That's the way people like him are. They stir things up with false suspicions just to upset innocent people."

Chimlyn was challenged by his truck driving career. He'd been driving more than he was legally supposed to and sleeping in his lonely truck, but he never got used to it. The people he worked for always wanted him to drive farther on less sleep. If he got sick, he had to drive anyway.

He drove between Minnesota and California and was away from home for two weeks at a shot, usually lost in his thoughts. He had a cell phone, but reception was spotty in many areas. He also couldn't call oftentimes because Robin's nursing home restricted employee phone usage. If he didn't catch her on break at 11:20 in the morning, he had to wait until that evening to hear her voice. There was plenty to be angry about on the road, but not being able to talk to Robin pissed him off the most.

He lived in his thoughts because they sustained him during the long lonely hours. If absence made the heart grow fonder, it made Chimlyn very, very fond. Robin was his life's focus. He counted the days until they would again be together, and the two or three days they spent together went by much too quickly.

He'd get home, relax a bit, then start on his "honey do" list. Then, before he had time to blink, he was back on the road again. Robin constantly asked him to quit, but he couldn't. They had decided to work extra hours so they could save for a used car and a down payment on a house. They had both grown up in Madelia and knew it would be a great place to raise a family.

Chimlyn wanted to do well by his Robin, but if he quit trucking, he had no idea what else he could do. Robin was determined to find out how much the capital pictures were worth. If it was enough, they could finally start the life they had been dreaming of for so long.

Chimlyn still liked his Popular Mechanics, but he didn't read much else. After graduating, his fear of being stupid had faded. Adults didn't pick on each other like kids did. However, he still felt he wasn't as smart as most folks.

Ma had always told him that everything happens for a reason and that god had made him like he was, but god never seemed to hear Chimlyn's prayers for help, so he eventually quit praying to be smarter and started accepting things the way they were. One of the things he was very thankful for was having a smart uncle like Lobs.

Chimlyn liked to swing by Lobs's house whenever he had a chance. In the evening, Lobs would be in the backyard enjoying the fading sunlight while sipping Old Crow bourbon on the rocks. They'd laugh and talk. Lobs thought it was hilarious that Chimlyn was an over-the-road trucker but couldn't stomach good whiskey. It made him gag, so Chimlyn stuck to his beer.

Lobs liked to remind Chimlyn, "You've got a good woman, a good job, and your health. Just you never forget it."

Talk like that helped Chimlyn believe that if he just stuck to it, things would eventually work out. He was always happy to see Madelia coming into view through his windshield. It was a good town, and the last time anyone had suffered any fatal violence was when the townspeople had caught up with the Jesse James gang and put an end to the Younger brothers. Everyone knew everyone and no one had to lock their doors at night.

One day as he was entering the city limits, Chimlyn decided to stop into a cafe for their early bird special before going home and getting some sleep. Robin was at work, so he didn't have to go home right away. He could get something to eat and catch up on the local gossip at the same time.

"Hi, Chim," said his friend Bobby as he flopped down in a booth across from Chimlyn.

Bobby White had always been good company and had attended some of the Barn parties before leaving town for South Central Technical College. Bobby had studied furnace repair and had done well for himself. He even had a van that read: Bob White Heating and Cooling—No Job too Big or too Small.

Bobby then lowered his voice and asked, "I hate to ask, Chim, but are you and Robin still together?"

"Well, sure," Chimlyn replied. "She's working down at the nursing home right now."

Bobby looked around, then said in a conspiratorial whisper, "Christ, Chim, I know that! I mean are you two still together—like in still married?"

"What the hell are you talking about, Bobby?" Chimlyn asked. "Last time I checked, I was still married. You wanna tell me what you're driving at?"

"Well, Coleen wanted to rent that Johnny Depp movie about pirates, so she headed for Kwik Trip," Bobby explained. "While she was there, she saw Robin with some older guy who wasn't from around here."

While Chimlyn looked at him in surprise, Bobby continued, "Look, Chim, I just thought I should tell ya. I know you'd do the same for me. I just didn't want you hearing it through the grapevine, you know? You know how Coleen likes to talk, and before long it'll be all over town."

Chimlyn just stared at his friend in disbelief. "Are you sure about this? Coleen must have been wrong."

"I hope so, man, I really do," said Bobby. "I'm just telling you what Coleen told me. She says they didn't see her, but they got into a car and drove away."

Then, after an uncomfortable silence, Bobby cleared his throat and changed the subject. "Hey, who are the Vikings playing this week? Guess it don't matter much. They're gonna get their asses handed to them, don't ya think?"

When Chimlyn just stared off into space, Bobby shrugged his shoulders, said he had to hit the road, then headed for the cash register. Chimlyn didn't even notice. Coleen must have been mistaken. Married people didn't mess around. The priest was always talking about scary things that happened to people who disrespected their vows.

None of what Bobby had just told him made any sense and he refused to believe it, but even so, Chimlyn was scared. It would hurt way too much to find out that Robin was hugging and kissing and acting lovey-dovey with another guy.

He finished eating and headed for home. After he pulled into the garage, he left everything in the car and marched into the house. He rifled through the garbage, getting coffee grounds all over his sleeves, but he didn't care. He found a torn-up piece of paper with a time and phone number on it, along with the word "Badge." He stuffed the paper into his pocket.

Then he booted up their computer and checked the history bar on the Google home page. Nothing looked suspicious, but Robin had apparently been checking for information about a cop named Martin McMurphy who had started taking drugs or something.

Another guy in the report was named Chief Charles Pullet. There were pictures of him talking to reporters, using cop words like "evidence," "Oxycontin," "data practices," and "unpaid administrative leave." Why would Robin want to know about that? "Badge" must mean something, but what?

He hoped to get some sleep before Robin got home so they could talk about it. Coleen was the town gossip, but she might have seen something, even though Robin had always sounded perfectly normal on the phone.

His heart pounding, Chimlyn dialed the number on the slip of paper. A man answered, "Badge here. May I help you?" Chimlyn was silent long enough that the voice said, "Chief Pullet here. May I help you?" When there was another long silence, Badge said, "Oh, I'm sorry. I see from the caller ID that it's you, Mrs. Madelia. Would you like to get together and try it again?"

Although there was no way Chimlyn could have known it, Badge's comment about "trying it again" was in regard to their trip to the state capital.

Chimlyn's heart was now in his throat. Robin had let that man do things to her! He was filled with rage, pain, and remorse, all at the same time. If he hadn't been on the road all the time, it never would have happened. He was sick and tired of being made to always having to feel bad about who and what he was.

Without a word, Chimlyn hung up the phone and again stared off into space for a long time. Then he returned to the computer to read more of the news reports Robin had been reading. Badge was a man, it was his phone number on the note, and something was up between that man and his beloved Robin.

By the time Robin finally walked into the living room, Chimlyn had fallen asleep while sitting on the couch. As she gently shook him, she told him she was glad he was home and that she would help him to bed. Nothing seemed out of the ordinary.

Confused, Chimlyn looked up at his wife and asked softly, "Do you still love me the way you're supposed to?"

Robin looked surprised as she said, "What? Of course I do. What are you talking about?"

"I'm talking about a police chief who likes you," Chimlyn said flatly. "A police chief that you've been with while I was gone."

Robin was speechless. How had Chimlyn found out? All her pain and guilt came rushing at her, but she didn't know what to do about it.

"Look, I need some time to sort some things out," Robin finally said. "Can I leave Peachy with you for a little while?"

Robin's response took Chimlyn completely by surprise. "You don't have to go," he said plaintively. "I got ya a present when I was in California, and I wanna give it to ya. You won't be with that other guy again, right?"

Robin smiled wanly, then again asked Chimlyn to take care of Peachy. She said she'd think things over and get together with him after Halloween, which was only two days away.

"I'm gonna stay at Nightingale's house. I work with her."

"I know," Chimlyn said, "but why are you leaving so fast? I don't get it."

Robin didn't know how to save a marriage which meant everything to her, so she was eager to run away from her problems until she had time to think. Chimlyn only knew that the man who called himself Badge had stolen something precious and that it filled him with rage.

Her encounter with Badge had made Robin feel like something vile after Badge had finished defiling her. She had even taken her wedding ring off and was soaking it in bleach. She had tried to be something she wasn't, and now she was paying the price. It was a horrible situation, and somehow it just had to be her fault. Now she needed time to sort it all out, once and for all.

Robin knew only one thing for certain. She had trusted a policeman who had turned out to be a wolf in sheep's clothing.

—CHAPTER 11—

ABDUCTION
"Suicide Solution" (Ozzy Osbourne)

Things in Normal were looking up for Badge. Martin's name was being smeared in the headlines, he was on unpaid leave, and he was facing the full wrath of the court system. Badge figured Martin would be headed down the road before long.

However, Sassy had kept calling, wanting to stay on top of what she called "the Martin problem."

She would say things like, "Look, Badge, if I told you once, I've told you a million times. I want Martin all gone bye-bye. Why is that man still on my school board?"

There was no doubt about it. Sassy scared the hell out of Badge, but there was very little he could do about the situation. He had essentially removed Martin from the police department, but he had no authority to interfere with the school board. Sassy knew that as well as he did, but she kept harassing him, and Badge couldn't understand why.

On the bright side, Badge's gonorrhea had cleared up to the point where he could relieve himself without wanting to scream in agony. He hoped Sassy had been infected. It would have served her right.

Agnes was almost back to where she had been before her talk with Mrs. Alaska's husband, although Badge had started keeping his off-duty weapon at work so she wouldn't be tempted to kill herself again. He hadn't been able to hook up with Mrs. Alaska, but there would be others to use for his pleasure.

Then out of the blue, Robin texted Badge from Madelia. He knew it was her because her number came up on his caller ID. Badge's imagination conjured a million delightfully filthy thoughts. He figured she probably wanted to hook up again, this time in a sober condition. He also wondered briefly if he had given her the clap. He wasn't eager to get it again.

Even so maybe Mrs. Madelia would be just what the doctor ordered. He needed a little pokey time to take his mind off Martin, Sassy, Agnes, Mrs. Alaska, and all the other bothersome things in his life. He could hook up with Robin and forget everything—at least for awhile.

Looking at his phone, Badge read Robin's text message: *Wanna get together? I can come to Normal. Meet in the back of Oak Wood Cemetery. Let's try it again. ;)*

He grew hard over her obvious desire to see him—this time without any pretext. She had even added a wink to the end of her text! Would she let him polish her ring again? He had to find out. She wanted to meet him the day before Halloween in a cemetery! It was too kinky to be true. Would she really want it in the cemetery? Just the thought made him even harder.

Agnes had never questioned Badge's activities since the phone call, and she soon slipped back to her old ways. No mention was ever made of counseling sessions to make their marriage better. She made herself believe Badge's stories, even though she had begun to realize what all his conventions were really about.

Badge was sexually charged as he swung his car into the cemetery. He'd park in the back by the woods along the river. It was getting colder at night and winter would be showing up soon, but Badge rolled down the window to let in some musky autumn air. He was a bit annoyed that Mrs. Madelia had wanted to meet so early in the day. On the other hand, they'd both get laid and then go their separate ways.

The cemetery was deserted. Badge hummed to himself as he sat in the car and waited. Then a car swung into the cemetery. Was it Robin? No, it was big fella—probably someone coming to take flowers off a grave, since they needed to be removed before the snow fell. Regardless, it meant that there would be no screwing in the cemetery. It just wouldn't work. It was just too risky. They'd have to get a motel room to take care of their lascivious business.

The car slowed and the big guy climbed out. He was a younger man, and he smiled at Badge as he lumbered toward a gravesite carrying a yellow flower in his hand.

Badge looked away, intently scanning the cemetery for a car with a young lady in it. A moment later, he felt a handgun pressed against his left temple. Badge cursed himself for letting his lust impair his observational skills. The man had walked right up to the car and was now threatening him.

"Put your hands into this or die, asshole!" Chimlyn ordered menacingly, thrusting a long plastic loop through the window.

Slipping one end of the plastic into the other end made the plastic act like handcuffs. Badge complied wordlessly. Once Badge's hands were bound, the young man reached into the vehicle and removed his gun from its holster. Chimlyn then opened the glove compartment and froze at the sight of the pink panties, recognizing them as a pair he had given Robin for Christmas. He reached out, grabbed the panties, and thrust them into the pocket of his jacket.

His rage rising, Chimlyn tore open the door and pulled Badge from the squad car. Then he shoved him into the backseat of his own car and bound the chief's legs with another plastic cable tie. After securing Badge's legs, he forced him to the floor and covered him with a blanket.

Slamming the door shut, he stormed back to the front seat, fired up the engine, and drove away. As he lay helpless in the darkness of the backseat, Badge tried to understand what had just happened. Was the man Mrs. Alaska's husband? His fear continued to rise as Chimlyn's car rumbled along the road.

Chimlyn had always hated having people ask him questions that caused him to think. He didn't trust how he thought about people, places, or things. People made him nervous, so he'd just smile when others were arguing with each other. Sometimes he'd nod and flash an enigmatic smile, but he rarely dared to add more than a word or two.

Decision making could also be hard for Chimlyn. When shopping, Robin was a big help. She could always spot the best deals. Robin was good to him and he knew it. He liked how she made him laugh and settle down when he was agonizing over things other folks never seemed to struggle with.

They had stood in front of a priest and promised god that they would always be married. Then Bob White had told him that Coleen had seen Robin with a stranger. He had gotten even more worried when he found a slip of paper in the wastebasket. Then he discovered that Robin had taken off her wedding ring, and when he asked her to explain everything, she had walked out, saying that she needed to think things over.

Chimlyn had set the meeting for early in the morning so no one would be in the cemetery. He knew Badge would be waiting for Robin—and he also knew that there had been something between them. Why else would two people meet in a cemetery?

The gun Chimlyn had shoved against Badge's temple wasn't loaded. He was mad at Badge, but he'd had no desire to hurt him, much less kill the man. He had bought the plastic cable ties at Home Depot because he had no idea where a person could buy handcuffs. Then he had stopped at Fleet Farm and bought a crossbow and three arrows, along with the single yellow flower.

Badge's fear rose with each passing mile. He was helpless and confused. How could it all have happened so fast? He'd been waiting for pleasure to arrive in the shape of a small-town girl, and now some insane bastard had hog-tied him and was planning—what? He didn't know, but it couldn't be good. He realized that as much as he hated the car ride, he was going to despise arriving at the destination even more. Finally, he hit upon a plan.

"My wrists hurt," he whined from the backseat. "Can you loosen these things a little?"

"I'm hurting, too," Chimlyn replied, "so just keep a lid on it, you son of a bitch. You got caught with your dick in the cookie jar, so if I were you, I'd keep my big mouth shut!"

Since his first idea had failed, Badge began to work on a new plan. What could he do to convince this clown to let him go? The man was obviously unbalanced or he never would have risked kidnapping a chief of police. That also meant that he was capable of extreme violence, so Badge needed to be careful not to provoke him.

After what seemed like forever, Badge felt the car slow down, then come to a stop. Then he heard what seemed to be a garage door shutting from overhead. A few moments later, he was being hoisted out of the car. As the blanket was pulled away from his head, Badge realized that he was now sitting in a chair at the table of the same robin's egg blue kitchen he'd seen before.

Chimlyn quickly fastened Badge securely into the chair with more plastic cable, then turned toward the kitchen counter. Badge recoiled in horror as Chimlyn turned back toward him, holding a knife in his right hand.

Terror-stricken, Badge watched as Chimlyn walked slowly toward him. "Look, I'm only gonna ask this once," Chimlyn said. "I need you not to scream and carry on. Do you understand?"

Badge nodded vigorously, then asked as calmly as possible, "Wh—what are you doing to me? Whatever's bothering you, I can explain."

Chimlyn said nothing as he took the knife and began to cut off Badge's shirt. When he had finished, he put the knife back in the drawer. Badge breathed a huge sigh of relief, since it appeared that the insane man wasn't going to kill him or cut off his balls.

Chimlyn then took a permanent marker from another drawer, then walked back to Badge and drew a black heart on Badge's chest, complete with an arrow piercing it. When he finished his drawing, he stepped back to admire his handiwork.

"There, I just made a nice target for me to aim at," Chimlyn said matter-of-factly.

As the realization of what was about to happen washed over him, Badge said frantically, "Look, if we have a misunderstanding or something, I think we can clear things up."

It was the only weapon left in Badge's survival arsenal: a shitload of lies. He had to figure out what the madman wanted to hear. It was the only thing that could save him. Badge sat helplessly as Chimlyn pushed his chair in front of the refrigerator. Chimlyn then left the kitchen for a few moments and returned carrying a crossbow and several arrows.

Chimlyn dragged another chair into position at the other end of the small kitchen and then used two C-clamps to secure the crossbow to its back, pointed directly at Badge's chest. He then loaded the crossbow with an arrow and began cranking it into firing position with a wrench of some sort. As Chimlyn continued to methodically set up his equipment, Badge began to weep like the frightened child he had always been.

He had lied, become a cop, and had sex with multiple women because he hadn't wanted to be Mother's darling little invisible boy. Agnes had been a constant reminder of how Mother pushed him around. There was no hiding—and not even his badge could save him now.

Paying no attention to Badge's pleas, Chimlyn began filling a bucket with water. Another empty bucket had been attached to the crossbow's trigger after passing over the back of the chair. The second bucket, now filled, had a hole in it that Chimlyn had plugged with a cork containing an eye screw. The full bucket was then placed on the kitchen counter above the empty one. Chimlyn strung nylon rope through the eye screw and then tied it to Badge's left index finger.

Badge said, "Listen, we've got to talk this out. You don't look like a bad guy, and I don't think you'd hurt a guy with a family. I've got a little boy and a girl, and they're great kids. Do you have kids? I'm supposed to take them trick-or-treating tomorrow. How about you?"

Wordlessly, Chimlyn sat on the floor with his back against the wall and admired his handiwork. If Badge pulled on the nylon rope, the cork would pop out of its hole, the water would fill the bucket dangling below the first pail, and when it got heavy enough it would pull the trigger and the crossbow would drive its arrow into Badge's black heart. When the crossbow finally fired, Chimlyn planned to look away, even though he knew it was fair and had to happen to make things right.

Then something dawned on him. The arrow would pass right through Badge and might ruin something in the kitchen. He got up, walked out to the garage, cut a sheet of plywood in half, and then propped it behind Badge's chair. That would absorb the impact and stop anything bad from happening.

Beads of sweat running down his forehead, Badge asked, "Why are you doing this? What did I ever do to you? Do I even know you? I'm a police officer. It's my job to *help* people. I can help you understand if you'll only let me."

Chimlyn's eyes narrowed as he said, "You do things you shouldn't do. You say you've got kids, but you still do bad things. I can't put much stock in any guy who'd do the stuff you do."

"This is all a misunderstanding," Badge said, his voice trembling. "Let's straighten this out so we can put it behind us, okay?"

Chimlyn looked directly into Badge's frightened eyes. "I suggest you pray to god—and make it good—because as soon as you tug on that rope you're gonna be seein' him face-to-face."

Badge started crying even harder and begged, "I want to live! I want to be a good daddy for my babies. I don't want to die. Please, I'm begging you to let me go. My wife has muscular dystrophy, the Jerry Lewis thing. She needs me—and my babies need me. If you don't care about me, think about my wife and kids."

Badge had no idea that his lies were only digging his grave deeper. He would have been much better off if he had kept his mouth shut, but he simply couldn't. Finally, the room lapsed into utter silence, except for Badge's pitiful weeping.

Chimlyn knew he couldn't shoot a pigeon, let alone a human being, no matter how despicable that person might have been. Why didn't Badge pull the rope and get it over with himself? He didn't have all day. Robin would be getting off work at 5:00.

The silence was broken by the sound of the front doorbell. Badge immediately screamed for help, but Chimlyn quickly stood, grabbed a kitchen towel from the side of the sink, and stuffed it into Badge's mouth. Then he stomped into the living room to check on the door. When he returned, he looked even angrier.

"It was the damned bird," he growled. "That Peachy can imitate all kinds of things. He can do siren noises, the cuckoo clock, and all sorts of other stuff."

He reached out and removed the towel from Badge's mouth, saying, "Look, you're a cop. You do brave stuff all the time, so why don't you be brave now and just pull the rope? You know ya did bad and haveta make it good. I don't got all day. You won't hardly feel nothin'. God won't be mad for you for killing yourself because it'll actually be the water bucket that will kill ya. All you gotta do is pull the rope."

Badge just stared at Chimlyn in helpless silence. No more words would come—not even his precious lies. He was cornered and there were no options. For several more long moments, the room was deathly quiet.

As he sat waiting, Chimlyn began to have second thoughts. If he let Badge go, could he trust him not to tell anyone like he had said earlier? He stood and left the kitchen to sort through his rambling thoughts. He walked over to Peachy's cage, remembering that Robin had asked him to clean it. Even though Chimlyn didn't like birds, he loved Robin, so he would do as she asked.

Chimlyn opened the cage by snapping a clothespin off the door to let Peachy out so he could stretch on the tall stand to which the bird was tethered so he wouldn't fly all over the house. He then rolled up the newspapers on the bottom of the cage, cleaned the food bowls, and wiped down the cage bars. Robin was going to be proud of him when she got home.

Cleaning the cage was a welcome diversion, but when Chimlyn returned Peachy to the cage, he forgot to snap the clothespin onto the door.

—CHAPTER 12—

DISCUSSIONS
"Operator" (Jim Croce)

When Chimlyn was done with his cleaning up, his mind returned to the problem sitting out in the kitchen. He decided he needed help.

He thought, "I know! I'll call that guy Badge kicked off the police department for eating drugs. Maybe he can tell me what to do. I'll just tell Badge that he'd better give me the guy's phone number or else I'll give the rope a tug."

Chimlyn walked into the kitchen, yanked the towel out of Badge's mouth, and demanded, "What's that cop's name you kicked off the department—the guy in the computer?"

"Martin, uh, McMurphy, why?" Badge replied tentatively.

"Because I wanna know, that's why," Chimlyn said sternly. "What's his phone number?"

Badge gave Chimlyn the number, then Chimlyn stuck the towel back into his mouth. He was nervous about talking to a cop he'd never met before, but Chimlyn just knew Martin would give him the help he needed.

Chimlyn walked back out to the living room and dialed the number Badge had given him. He had even used Badge's phone so nothing could be traced back to him. After ringing three rings, Martin answered the phone.

After taking a deep breath, Chimlyn said, "Hello. I can't tell you my name and you don't know me, but I know how bad Chief Badge treated you."

At first, Martin was speechless, but he soon found his voice. "Well, kiss my ass and call me Jack. Who the hell is this? Oh, that's right, you're not going to tell me. If you're a reporter, just quote me as saying that Badge made a mistake by forgetting what it means to be a patrolman. He screwed up, but he's not man enough to admit it."

Chimlyn listened intently, then asked, "Well, would the world be a better place if Badge was gone? How would his wife and kids get along if he left them—for good? Isn't his wife really sick?"

Again Martin found himself without words for a few moments. "Agnes, that's his wife, isn't sick, unless you call eating too much a disease—and they don't have any kids." Then it suddenly occurred to Martin that maybe Badge had something to do with the call. "Look, is there something specific you need from me? Has Badge done something to hurt you?"

"He's hurt a lot of folks, I think," Chimlyn said thoughtfully. "I know he breaks God's rules and he lies. I'm thinking that nobody really likes him very much, do they?"

Playing for time, Martin kept up his line of questioning. "How did Badge hurt you?"

"I—I don't wanna say," Chimlyn mumbled.

"I understand," Martin said, his police training coming to life. "Look, would you like to meet and talk about all this?"

Chimlyn told Martin he'd call right back, then hung up. He needed time to think. He was confused and wanted to make the right decision, especially today, of all days. One thing he knew for sure: He was even madder at Badge than he had been before.

Walking back into the kitchen, Chimlyn said fiercely, "You liar! You don't have a sick wife, and you ain't got no kids at all! If you keep lying, you're going to hell. Shame on you! You make me sick!"

For a long several minutes, Chimlyn paced the kitchen floor, trying to decide what to do next. Finally, he walked back to the living room and dialed Martin's number again, but in his anger he used his own phone. When Martin answered, Chimlyn started talking while rubbing his eyes and forehead. As he talked, Chimlyn didn't hear Peachy pry open his cage—because Chimlyn had forgotten to secure it with the clothespin that usually held the door closed.

Peachy fluttered into the kitchen and landed on the kitchen counter as Badge watched in horror. The crossbow was cocked and ready to plunge its arrow into his heart. Then Peachy flapped his wings and lifted into the air briefly—coming to rest on the nylon rope that was the key to whether Badge would live or die.

Peachy flapped his wings as he attempted to grasp the rope with his claws. The rope grew taut, then the cork popped free from the pail. Badge screamed, but there was very little sound—surely not enough to be heard in the next room. Water began to pour into the pail, signaling his doom. Struggling frantically, Badge knew he was going to die—right there and then.

Peachy, tired of trying to balance on the rope, flapped toward the chair and landed next to the crossbow. After what seemed like forever, the pail obtained enough weight to fire the arrow, sending the chair it was mounted on crashing to the floor from the force of the release. Peachy squawked and took to the air as the dull thud of a projectile impaling plywood after plunging through flesh, bone, cartilage, and a human heart filled the air.

Hearing the commotion, Chimlyn dropped the phone and ran into the kitchen. Badge was still propped up in the chair, but there was an arrow in the middle of the heart that Chimlyn had drawn on his chest. A pulsing geyser of crimson was shooting from the wound, but its speed was decreasing as Badge's heart began to wind down.

Chimlyn just stood and stared for a long moment, his mouth wide open. Badge's head had drooped toward his chest, but his eyes looked like they could still see. Why hadn't his eyes closed like they did on TV whenever somebody died?

Chimlyn stood in awe as blood began to trickle from Badge's mouth and nostrils. He had no first-hand knowledge of dying. At least it had happened so fast that Badge probably hadn't felt any pain. Only then did Chimlyn notice that Peachy had flown up to the top of the refrigerator and was looking down on the death scene with interest.

"Bad bird!" Chimlyn shouted. "You should have stayed in your cage."

Peachy just sat where he was, unconcerned.

Then Chimlyn remembered the phone. He raced back to the living room and discovered that Martin was still there. Had he heard what had just taken place?

Indeed, Martin had heard a commotion, but had no idea what was going on. He had heard the man yell something about a peach or something—but he had also used the words *bad bird*. None of it made the slightest sense.

"I didn't do it!" Chimlyn blurted into the phone. "Peachy did it! Oh, god, what should I do now?"

Martin was confused, but immediately realized that the entire situation had changed. "Look, let's talk," he said calmly. "I've got nothing but time. Grab a glass of water or something and let's figure this out together, okay?"

Chimlyn sighed deeply and said, "Sometimes accidents happen.

That darn Peachy went and killed Badge. It wasn't me. You know it's true, right? I was talking to you on the phone when it happened."

"Whoa, whoa!" Martin said. "Slow down! What do you mean, the bird killed Badge?"

"Yeah," Chimlyn replied simply. "Should I call the cops or what?"

When Martin prodded for more details, Chimlyn began to pour out his story. He didn't know if he could trust anyone anymore, but he had to tell someone. It was like a dam had burst, and for several minutes, the words came rushing out until the entire incredible story had been told.

When Chimlyn finally wound down, Martin said, "Look, I don't know what's going on there, but you need to protect yourself."

Martin's words made Chimlyn feel a little better. He had stood up for himself, and now the evil Badge was gone and it would be up to God to decide what to do with him.

"Man, you still there?" Martin asked insistently when there was a long silence on the phone.

Chimlyn said, "Yeah, I'm still here."

"Good," said Martin. "You can talk to your priest about this maybe, but *not* the police. Clean everything up and never tell a living soul about what happened there today. Nobody! If you want to talk to me some more, you've got my number—but can you do me a favor?"

"What is it?" Chimlyn asked.

"Now that I've helped you, could you help me?" Martin asked, keeping his tone as light as possible. "If you can, please send me his badge. It'll be in his wallet. I want to make sure no one ever finds it. You just take care of cleaning everything up there and I'll make sure that badge disappears forever, okay?"

After taking down Martin's address, Chimlyn hung up the phone, grateful for how eager Martin had been to help him sort it all out. He went into the kitchen and felt around in Badge's pants pockets until he found the wallet. He pulled out the badge and stuffed it into his own pants pocket for safekeeping.

Then Chimlyn held up his arm and Peachy immediately flew down and landed on it, squawking, "Good Peachy! Peachy get a treat."

"Yeah," said Chimlyn, smiling for the first time since he had entered the kitchen, "you're a good bird. In fact, you're gonna get a couple treats today."

Lacy had been sitting nearby in the McMurphy house and had overheard Martin's end of the conversation. "What in the world was that all about?" she asked.

"Some guy's in big trouble," Martin replied flatly. "I guess Badge finally messed with the wrong guy's wife."

When Lacy pressed for more information, Martin added, "It sounds like there was some sort of accident, but I'm pretty sure Badge is dead. I don't know how it happened, but somehow there was a bird involved. It's pretty confusing, but I really think Badge is dead."

"Well, I hate to say it, but it serves the bastard right," Lacy said, surprising even herself with that statement. Martin was not surprised by his response, "That guy on the phone didn't like Badge messing around with his wife, so he did something about it—which no one had ever done before when it came to Badge. If he decides to come clean, a bunch of lawyers will swoop down and put him away forever, which somehow just doesn't seem right. We're always preaching to kids about Stranger Danger. Why don't we preach about Police Perils or something like that?"

"The guy wouldn't have a chance," Martin said. "They'd ask him if he actually saw Badge screw his wife, and when the guy said no, it would be ruled hearsay or some bullshit like that. The system wins and an innocent guy loses—it happens all the time. Look what the system did to you and me. It's *just this*—not justice! All I know is that it'll feel great tossing that damn badge into the shitter where it belongs!"

Lacy was quiet for a long time, then said, "Okay. I guess you and I will be going to Farmers Community Park together. We'll wipe Badge out of our lives when we toss that disgusting piece of metal into the park's outhouse—exactly where it belongs."

Martin took his wife in his arms, kissed her gently, and said, "You know something, Mrs. McMurphy? I love you."

Settling into her husband's warm embrace, Lacy replied, "And I love you, Mr. McMurphy."

—CHAPTER 13—

CLEAN-UP
"Keep a-Knockin'" (Jim Croce)

The arrow had been driven into the three-quarter inch plywood with such force that it nearly had gone completely through. Chimlyn cut the cable ties that had secured Badge to his death chair. He then took Badge's by his sagging shoulders and wiggled him off the arrow that had been driven through his chest.

After popping the body off the arrow, Chimlyn lowered it to the tarp. Then he dug under the sink and found a pair of latex gloves. He was glad he had thought of putting a tarp under the chair. There was blood from hell to breakfast.

Now that he had a dead guy lying on the kitchen floor, he began to feel his first pangs of doubt. His heart was racing and something about the whole thing no longer felt as right as it had before he had carried out his plan. He knew Badge was gone, but he was talking on the phone when Peachy triggered the contraption, so he hadn't killed anyone. So why was Martin telling him not to say anything about today?

Martin had told him that fish get caught because they open their mouths. He'd also said that innocent people are found guilty all of the time, which made Chimlyn even more scared and confused. He had called lawyers *legal eagles*, talking about how they didn't bat an eye over putting innocent people away.

The kitchen smelled horrible, and Chimlyn had never been around so much blood, but there was no other choice but to get everything cleaned up before Robin got home. She would never understand this. He wasn't sure he even understood it anymore.

Suddenly, the doorbell rang, sending waves of sheer panic through Chimlyn's soul. He quickly used a part of the tarp to cover the messy corpse. For several long moments, Chimlyn found himself unable to move. He just stood frozen with his mouth wide open.

"God, if it's Robin, I'm screwed." Chimlyn mumbled. "Or what if it's Ma and Pa? What can I tell 'em?"

There were so many questions, but no answers. He began walking zombie-like toward the living room, sweating profusely. Even though he had entered that room thousands of times, he somehow kicked over a table lamp sending it crashing to the wooden floor. Now there was no chance that whoever was at the door would believe no one was home. He had to answer.

He walked to the window and peeked through the drapes. He saw a short bald guy with a beer belly standing at the door in a dark brown UPS uniform. Chimlyn breathed a huge sigh of relief. UPS guys never came into the house. They just had you sign for stuff and then left.

Chimlyn walked over and opened the door. "Hello," he said as nonchalantly as he could. "Sorry it took so long to answer. What have you got for me?"

"Unless you're Robin Johnson, I have nothing for you," the heavy man replied.

"Oh, okay," said Chimlyn, "but I am her husband."

The UPS man smiled and said, "I don't believe that will be a problem. You can just sign for her."

"Good," Chimlyn said, taking the pen from the UPS man's hand and scribbling his name. "Thank you. You can go now."

As he was turning to leave, the UPS man pointed toward the floor of the living room and said, "Man, you'd better clean that up before your wife gets home!"

Chimlyn looked back and was horrified to see a trail of brownish-red footprints across the floor. His heart in his throat, he said, "Oh, my gosh! You're right. My wife's gonna kill me!"

Chimlyn closed the door and looked at the box the UPS man had handed him. Robin would never know that whatever she'd bought on eBay had nearly given him a heart attack. He wondered if the UPS guy had been able to tell it was blood on the floor. Only time would tell.

As he set the box on an end table and returned to the kitchen, a plan started forming in Chimlyn's mind. He started cleaning up, and as he scrubbed, he even hummed a little. The work helped push the fear and confusion out of his thoughts.

He pulled out the plastic tarp by its sides. Badge's eyes were half open, like the eyes of someone trying to stay awake while watching a movie on late-night TV, but it was the smell that bothered Chimlyn most. Badge had apparently filled his pants at the moment of death, and the soggy excrement seeping through Badge's jeans almost pushed Chimlyn's stomach to force its contents out immediately. He put an ice cream bucket next to him, just in case. He didn't need still another mess to clean up. As he continued cleaning, he saw that Badge had also pissed his pants. It brought him even closer to losing his lunch.

In spite of the grossness of the sights and smells, Chimlyn worked slowly and meticulously. He wanted the awfulness out of his kitchen and out of his life, but he also knew he'd have to be careful. He rolled the body up in the tarp and tied it carefully with rope from the garage.

Before dragging the dead weight out the kitchen door and into the garage, he looked back to survey the scene. The floor was clean, but the plywood backstop was smeared with blood. He couldn't leave that lying around the garage. Robin would surely ask questions. He would get rid of that when he disposed of Badge's body.

Then he thought about the crossbow and arrows. He decided to toss them into the river, along with everything else—but would they float? He couldn't take that chance, so he stuffed the crossbow and arrows into a potato sack to get rid of separate from the body. The cops might somehow be able to trace the bow and arrows to him. He was glad when the corpse finally stopped making strange noises each time he moved it.

While sliding the tarp into the garage, he stumbled once, but besides that, it had been smooth sailing, except for a little leaking at the side of the tarp. It was a nuisance, but Chimlyn quickly cleaned it up and then tied more rope around the body to seal it more securely.

In the garage, Chimlyn opened the trunk of the car and lined it with old rugs. No sense fouling up the trunk with blood and the horrible smell. He could just toss those along with everything else.

When he had the trunk secure and was sitting behind the wheel of his car, Chimlyn was finally able to think about something besides the task at hand. Robin had said something about thinking things over and seeing him after Halloween. That was actually a good thing, in a weird way. He would have loved to see her, but not with a dead guy in the trunk.

"Have I forgotten anything?" he asked himself.

He got out of the car again and took a quick walk through the house to make sure everything was in order. It was approaching 5:00. Just as he was turning to go back out into the garage, the front doorbell rang again.

This time he was much more confident and relaxed as he walked over and peeked through the living room drapes. As he pulled the drapes back, he found himself staring into Robin's glaring eyes. She knew he would be peeking out before answering the door.

After the initial shock wore off, Chimlyn was actually relieved that it was Robin and not the cops—but why hadn't she just used her key?

When he opened the door, Robin said curtly that she hadn't wanted to dig around in her purse for the keys. Then she added that she needed to talk to him. She was also concerned about Peachy.

As she walked toward Peachy's cage, she commented on the awful smell in the room. She assumed Chimlyn had forgotten to clean Peachy's cage, although it had never smelled like this.

"Did you clean the cage like I told you?" she asked. "It smells like someone died in here."

"Yeah, I let him out so he could get some exercise," Chimlyn said. "I even gave him sunflower seeds for a treat. Oh, and you got an eBay box today. Is it a Halloween costume?"

Robin turned and looked directly into Chimlyn's eyes. "Chimlyn, you know I think the world of you and I want to do right by you," she said, knowing he was covering something up. He was easy to read, after all the time she'd known him. "Why don't you go and hang out with Lobs for awhile?"

Chimlyn followed Robin like a puppy as she walked around the house. She saw nothing out of the ordinary, but something was wrong.

Finally, she turned to him and demanded, "Chimlyn, out with it! You're up to something, and I wanna know what it is—now!"

As Robin crossed her arms and tipped her shoulders back, Chimlyn struggled to think of a response. Finally, something erupted deep in the dark recesses of his brain.

"Robin," he said firmly, "I'm gonna tell your folks how you treat me. We're married, and what you're doin' ain't right."

"I'll handle them," Robin said defensively. "Don't you worry about that."

Both of them were struggling mightily to level with each other, and in a strange quirk of irony, both their confessions would have involved Badge. It was a bizarre stand-off, and it was anyone's guess how it would end.

After a long uncomfortable pause, Chimlyn said softly, "Robin, you're my wife. You married me in front of God, so I think you should act like it. You said, 'Till death do us part,' and what would your parents think now? What would God think?"

Although Robin didn't know exactly what Chimlyn was trying to say, she felt a tear run down her cheek. She wiped it away and said, "Look Chimlyn, we really need to have a talk."

Robin found herself aching for Chimlyn to put his big strong arms around her, but she stood her ground, waiting for his reply. Chimlyn was aching for her touch, too, but he cleared his throat and looked away, saying, "I got some stuff to do first. Maybe we can meet for breakfast at Kwik Trip tomorrow."

"I'm not quite sure what you're talking about, Chimlyn," Robin said, wiping away another tear, "but I hope you believe that I'm not a bad person. I also hope you believe that I want to be with you—forever, just like we said in the church, in front of God and everyone else."

Chimlyn felt his heart leap at those words, but he still had things to take care of before he and Robin could start life fresh.

He wiped away a tear of his own, then turned toward the kitchen. There was no way to avoid what he had to do, even though it would hurt Robin at the moment. He made himself a promise that if she would agree to meet him the next morning, he'd never mention any of it again.

"Meet me tomorrow morning, Robin, please," Chimlyn said, barely able to look at his wife's tortured face.

There was another long pause, then Robin started toward the front door. "I'll think about it," she said. "I was hoping we could talk now, but I guess it's not a convenient time for you. Goodbye, Chimlyn."

With that, she walked out of the house, got into her Ford Falcon, and drove away. Chimlyn had no idea if he'd ever see his wife again. Chimlyn stood in the doorway, watching her taillights disappear in the distance. He didn't know it, but she'd only make it a couple blocks before she pulled over and parked, accompanied solely by her tormented thoughts.

Nothing had worked out the way he had planned. Peachy had killed Badge and now he had hurt Robin badly enough that she might never want to see him again. He briefly wondered if birds could burn in hell.

—CHAPTER 14—

CRUISING
"Takin' Care of Business" (Bachman-Turner Overdrive)

Chimlyn was in a faraway place, alone with his thoughts of pending doom, when the cuckoo clock in the living room sounded six times, pulling him back to the present moment. It was already dark outside. He had a bundle in the trunk that wasn't in a hurry to get anywhere, but it had to go somewhere. It was a disgusting chore, but he had to get it done.

As Chimlyn finally began his unpleasant task, his anger again flared. It was all the cop's fault—and now he had to bury his ugly, smelly body somewhere, dump it off a bridge, or something. Even dead, the guy was a thorn in his side. It just didn't seem fair.

In the garage, he tossed a shovel onto the backseat of the car. Then it dawned on him that he'd left the arrow in the sink after he'd rinsed it off. How could Robin have missed it? Had she seen it and not said anything?

He went back into the kitchen and retrieved the arrow. Then he backed the car out of the garage, deciding to head for the Watonwan

River bridge. As he drove down the street, he waved at a couple of neighbors who were strolling on the sidewalk. He was trying to be as cool as he always was—or at least trying not to look too suspicious.

He slowed for a red light, worried that a car full of kids was coming up from behind him too quickly. What if they rear-ended him and the trunk popped open? He sighed as they came to a smooth stop. As his mind raced, he was startled back to reality by the honk of a car horn. The light had changed and the kids were impatient. A moment later they passed him, one of them flipping him the bird as they drove by.

Chimlyn knew he was playing a deadly serious game with horrible consequences if he got caught. Lady Luck had been on his side so far—but there was no way he could know that his luck was about to run out and it was going to cost him dearly. It was nearly 6:30 when Chimlyn suddenly noticed that the gas gauge was on empty.

"Oh, man!" he growled, pounding on the steering wheel.

He made a U-turn and headed back east toward the Kwik Trip on Highway 169. He dug his wallet out and found only two lonely one-dollar bills. Two bucks wouldn't get him to his destination and back, but he couldn't head for Hanska to borrow some cash from his folks. One look at him and his mom would know something was up. He'd have to go back home and raid the piggy bank.

He made it home, picked up his change, and pulled into the Kwik Trip without running out of gas, but it was a white knuckle drive all the way. He breathed a huge sigh of relief as he jumped out of the car to pump the gasoline. As the gas started flowing, he noticed the arrow on the passenger seat and his heart started racing again—but it was about to race even faster.

Just as Chimlyn finished fueling up, a squad car pulled into the lot and parked near the front door. A cop got out and stood next to the car, adjusting his belt while trying to see himself in the reflection of the side window. He wanted to make sure he was looking good for the people of Madelia, but Chimlyn couldn't help wondering if there was a pretty young married woman in the store.

Looking closer, Chimlyn saw that the officer was Chief Frankie Fellows. He'd been a cop in Madelia for as long as Chimlyn could remember and was well respected in the community. Maybe all cops didn't go around chasing married women and getting them to break their vows.

After hauling his double-bagged stash of change into the store, Chimlyn heaved it onto the counter and started counting out the money for his twenty-dollar gas bill.

He actually jumped when he heard the chief say from behind him, "What did ya do, rob a bank, Chimlyn?"

"Oh, no," Chimlyn said, trying to be nonchalant. "It's money from the piggy bank. I didn't get a chance to hit the ATM today. I got gas."

As he went back to his counting, he could feel his face reddening.

Frankie laughed and said, "Oh, no, you got gas, take it outside. We can't have gassy customers in here."

"How much do you need, Chimlyn?" Chief Fellows asked. "I could loan it to you till you can get to the ATM."

"Twenty dollars. I have enough here," Chimlyn said softly, realizing that Frankie was only trying to be funny.

"Chicken feed," said the chief. "At least let me help you pile up the quarters so you can count quicker." As the chief began stacking quarters, he added, "How've you been?"

"I try to be good all the time," Chimlyn responded, instantly wondering why he had said it.

"You know, I used to love working your football games and watching you kick ass," said Chief Fellows. "I was one of your biggest fans and I was really sorry your playing days had to end like they did."

Then the chief said something that sent shivers down Chimlyn's spine. "You know, some folks would hate being a small town cop, but

I've always loved it. We haven't had a killing around here for over 100 years, when folks shot up the Younger boys after they robbed the Northfield bank with Jesse James. Nobody gets murdered in these parts and that's okay with me."

All Chimlyn could do was smile and nod as he kept counting out his change. When he had finally paid the bill, Chief Fellows even bought him a doughnut. It was one of the strangest things that had happened that day—and it had already been the strangest day of Chimlyn's life.

He jumped into the car and downed the doughnut in two bites. Then he waved goodbye to the chief and pulled out of the gas station. Maybe there were some good cops around after all. He had always liked Chief Fellows—but he wondered what the chief would think of him if he knew about the baggage in his trunk. He shuddered even to think about it.

He started wishing he had left the whole thing in God's hands. God probably would have done a better job of straightening Badge out than he had, but it was too late to worry about that. Now he had to clean up his mess and move on.

As he drove, Chimlyn thought about the hooker who was about to be stoned in the Bible. Jesus had told the people that whoever was without sin should throw the first stone. Chimlyn knew he wasn't perfect. He had messed up, but it had been an accident. He also knew that he couldn't come clean about what had happened that day, not even to Chief Fellows.

Then Chimlyn recalled a conversation he'd once had with Lobs. Although it had sounded funny at the time, by now it had turned into a scary memory. Lobs had told him essentially the same thing Martin McMurphy had said. He couldn't trust the government or the powers that be for fairness in this world. There were plenty of people who would gladly throw the first stone, whether they were sinful or not.

People conveniently forget the shenanigans they've pulled when it's time for a good stoning.

Then he recalled another story Lobs had told him. Lobs had said that people like to go to executions just to remind themselves that there are other people in the world who are having a worse day than they are.

Meanwhile, Robin was driving north on Hwy 169 toward Mankato, not going anywhere in particular and lost in her thoughts. She didn't want to go back to Nightingale's. She just wanted to be alone if she couldn't be with Chimlyn. She was feeling horrible about the grotesque life she was living. She had once felt clean, but now she felt filthy—and totally alone.

Her memory refused to let go of a night she desperately wanted to forget. She wished she could just die and not have to keep reliving those awful memories.

Chimlyn had never rejected her before. Was their marriage over? She simply didn't know. Being a divorcee sounded sinful. Robin knew that Chimlyn was kind-hearted and attentive, but how could she ask him to understand something she herself would never be able to understand?

The thing she remembered most about that night was Badge had pounded awful feelings into her, crushing all the beauty from her life. She had always been eager to wake up and meet her days, but she had lately found herself dreading having to drag herself out of bed after another night filled with remorse and fitful nightmares.

Chimlyn deserved better. Now he thought she was just a sleazy slut and didn't even want her in the house.

"Why did I ever believe that Badge?" she wailed, tears rolling down her cheeks. "I wish Chimlyn had never found those damned pictures."

She wondered how Chimlyn had found out about her and Badge. It was probably all over town. Maybe Badge had been bragging about taking advantage of a dim-witted slut.

Then something caught her eye, in spite of the tears that filled her eyes. She saw Chimlyn's car pulling out of the Kwik Trip parking lot.

—CHAPTER 15—

VOMIT
"Down by the Side of the Road" (John Prine)

Chimlyn felt a lot better about things. Frankie had turned out to be a good guy, the house was all cleaned up, and now all he had to do was dump the crossbow in the drink and tuck Stiff and Stinky in the shit pits for his dirt nap. It would be smooth sailing from that moment on.

The next day was Halloween, and Chimlyn found himself hoping he'd be able to hand out candy with Robin. Everything was going to be good again, just like before, now that Badge was gone.

Chimlyn was staring hard as he drove, but his eyes kept sliding shut. He was tired and hungry. A hamburger and warm bed would have been heaven for him at that moment, but he still had a hole to dig. The night was clear, dark, and chilly, but at least it wasn't raining. It was a perfect night to give Badge the type of burial he truly deserved.

As Robin followed Chimlyn from a safe distance, she was blinking away tears. "We should be together tonight," she was thinking, "I haven't changed, and I'm definitely not as bad as he thinks I am. I want things to be like they've always been."

As her tears flowed, Robin was hoping that when Chimlyn finally stopped they could talk and make things right. She didn't want to wait until morning. Life would have been so much easier if rotten guys like Badge weren't allowed to run around tricking dim-witted small town girls.

Chimlyn continued to battle sleep and hunger as he neared the shit pits. He wondered if he should take a quick cat nap before he began his task, but he couldn't risk being caught. No, he had to finish the job. Then he could go home and sleep peacefully. He desperately didn't want to mess it up after he'd already come so far. Everything was going according to plan. All he had to do was dig a hole, toss the arrows, and get home. He even thought it would probably be a good idea to go to church on Sunday and ask for forgiveness, just in case. Then everything would be good again.

He drove over the bridge, but there were young people, drinking like young people had been doing for as long as he could remember. He'd have to throw the sack and arrow into the river somewhere else. He used to hang out there himself, waiting for Robin to show up after closing the store. Those were sweet times, the salad days of his life. Robin was the prettiest thing he'd ever seen—and she was his girlfriend back then! If things worked out, he would try to make things like that again between Robin and himself.

Robin was still following her husband from a distance, wondering where in the world he could be headed. Her thoughts were very different as she crossed the bridge. She was filled with guilt, anger, shame, and fear, and she had never felt so filthy in her life.

Shortly after crossing the bridge, Chimlyn turned west on a gravel road. Robin wondered if he might be headed to Lobs' place. The first turn after the railroad tracks led to the shit pits, but he couldn't be going there. As she followed from a distance, terrible thoughts played peek-a-boo with her mind. The worst was if it was okay to wish that Badge was dead.

As he neared the foul-smelling cattail patch of swamp known to the locals as the shit pits, he slowed the car to roll across a set of little-used railroad tracks. The shit pits always stank because of the rotting chicken parts being pumped into the Watonwan River by the chicken processing plant. Even so, it was the perfect place to dump Badge's stinking body. It seemed fitting somehow and better yet, no one would see him do it.

Death arrived for Robin a few moments later, just as she started to cross the railroad tracks. She had momentarily lost sight of Chimlyn's taillights and was further distracted by wiping the tears from her eyes when a 120-ton locomotive smashed into the side of her Ford Falcon, crushing and twisting her car into a useless pile of scrap metal. Lost in her thoughts and misery, Robin never saw the train coming or heard the whistle. In that moment, Robin vanished from Chimlyn's life—except for the painful memories that would linger forever in his mind.

By the time the huge locomotive finally ground to a halt, the engineer had notified the company of the accident, referring to it as a "grade crossing mishap." The Union Pacific dispatcher in Mankato notified the Watonwan sheriff's office, which then dispatched deputies, an ambulance, and a volunteer fire department crew from Madelia.

Badge's death in mid-afternoon had been followed by Robin's death in the early evening of the same day. She died never knowing she'd gotten her wish—that Badge was dead.

Death arrives in many forms. Badge had been given the opportunity to stare at the mechanism of his death. He'd been given a chance to beg and lie before an arrow put him forever into past tense. Conniving until the end, he had been unable to escape Death's grasp.

On the other hand, Robin never knew what hit her. She'd been alive one second and dead the next. The end of Robin's life had been punctuated by the deafening crunch of grinding, twisting steel. Robin had been reduced to a pitiful mess of bloody pulp and broken bones.

Death takes everything we've ever been or ever wanted to be. People play games, pretending that the dead are in a better place, all the while breathing a secret sigh of relief that they're not dead themselves. Death is final and permanent—and the concept of time is useless.

An entire community would suddenly be forced to grapple with a ridiculous, senseless, stupid tragedy. At Robin's funeral they'd say things like, "She was such a beautiful girl, but they had to have a closed casket. They say it was the worst accident around here in twenty years."

Cops are drawn to the very things that shock and repulse people most, scenes that are probably better left unseen. But the force of morbid curiosity is strong, and it pulls cops into scenes of the ugliest nastiness imaginable. The excitement of gruesome events has always drawn people into careers like law enforcement or ambulance driving.

As word spread through Madelia that a car had been hit by a train, even cops who weren't dispatched to the scene responded. Kids jumped into their cars to go see the carnage. Madelia's newest officer, fresh out of the academy, heard the call on his cruiser radio and met Chief Frankie Fellows in a parking lot. A small town cop's beat is usually boring, so smart bank robbers, well aware of this, actually report fake plane crashes or other emergencies to draw cops away from their intended targets.

The new cop, Nick, asked the chief if he could go check out the accident, and Frankie agreed. Frankie was actually happy to hear the request, because it would give his newest officer a chance to see the grisly side of police work for the first time. It would be good experience, and he needed to cut his teeth on a fatal accident sooner or later.

"Go ahead," said the chief. "They'll need help with crowd control, if I know this town. Call me on the local channel if you need another hand out there."

Frankie had seen his share of death and mayhem and was perfectly content to hang out in town. He only hoped it wasn't someone from Madelia, where everyone knew everyone. At least it wouldn't be one of his kids. They long since graduated and headed for greener pastures.

He thought back to the last fatal out by the shit pits. A '68 Chevy pickup had gotten smoked by a freight train. Frankie had been alone that night and had been forced to walk along the tracks to find the driver, who'd gotten blasted out of the truck and washed downstream in a drainage ditch paralleling the tracks. It was awful, and not at all helped by the stench of the shit pits itself.

Later that night, he had run into a reporter with a camera from the *Mankato Free Press* and had to give a report of what had happened. "The sixty-eight-year-old male driver was alone in his Chevy pickup," Frankie had told the reporter in a formal tone, "and was pronounced dead at the scene. His name is being withheld pending notification of the next of kin."

He had given the cop talk perfectly, and it had given the reporter what he needed—enough information to get started on his story. Frankie was surprised, however, when he was on the front page the next day. It was the first time his picture had ever been in the paper.

So Frankie Fellows knew what they'd be doing at the scene of the accident. They'd be taking photographs and making measurements. Witnesses would be interviewed and victims checked for vital signs. It was always the same.

At the scene of Robin's accident, there was no need to check for vital signs. There was barely enough of her body left to tell if she had been a male or female. They got one clue by finding her purse alongside the tracks, identifying her as Robin Johnson. Both deputies on the scene knew she had worked at the Ben Franklin store that had just closed.

The other deputy working the scene, Deputy Florski, asked Nick, "You wanna get a hold of Fellows and have him swing out here so he can do the death notification? Robin's folks are in town from Arizona this week, visiting friends before winter hits."

Nick called Fellows and then walked back to where Florski was standing. As he approached, he saw that Florski was actually mumbling to himself.

"God can be so unfair and cruel at times. If this can happen to a pretty little thing like Robin, it could happen to anyone. Doesn't look like drinking was involved. How in the hell could she not have seen the damn train? It's just plain unfair."

Florski thought back to the first fatal accident he'd worked on. A young female had been thrown from her vehicle after rolling it off a highway. She hadn't been wearing a seatbelt and ended up hitting a mile marker post and being decapitated. He'd been given the gruesome duty of having to look for the head. He remembered praying that he wouldn't vomit when he found it, which would have made him look like a fool in front of the other officers.

When he came across the head, Florski could see the whitish bronchial tube dangling from the neck. As he picked up the head by the hair with one hand and tried to steady it with the other hand, the retching in his stomach began—and didn't stop until every last drop of stomach bile had been splattered onto the ground. That had all happened more than twenty years ago, but the memory was still as fresh as ever, and every fatal accident he worked retriggered all those terrible scenes in his mind.

When he saw Nick coming, Florski turned to him and said, "Remember, kid, we have to be thorough on these things. We can't miss anything. Don't *assume* anything. It's an election year and the sheriff is gonna want his face plastered all over the news. He'll make our lives miserable if we make him look bad here."

Nick couldn't believe what he was hearing. The scene monstrous and unbelievable, yet strangely captivating. He had seen grisly pictures at the academy and had heard instructors say that if you couldn't handle a little blood you didn't belong in law enforcement.

Nick was determined to stay tough and to push down any feeling that might make him look like less of a man. However, as he continued to stare at the carnage around him, he felt his stomach beginning to churn. Real life was much worse than pictures in text books or scenes on movie screens. The sights were accompanied by awful smells and textures. It was surreal and gut-wrenching, yet he couldn't seem to look away from the macabre remnants of what had once been a beautiful young lady.

Suddenly, it was all too much. It came on fast and overwhelmed him. He raced off into the darkness and vomited violently, then sagged against the side of his patrol car in a stupor for several minutes before his mind returned to the present moment.

He realized he'd just committed an unacceptable act by tossing his cookies, and something inside told him he'd never forget the colors, the textures, the smells, and the horrendous sights he was seeing at that moment. It would never leave him, no matter how long he lived.

As he looked up, he was horrified to see Florski approaching. "Nick, are you okay?" Florski asked.

"Yeah. I guess I must have the flu or something," Nick replied. "I've never felt anything like that before."

Florski smiled and patted Nick on the shoulder. "Sure, kid, I know exactly how you feel. I had that same flu when I worked my first fatality."

Then Florski turned to walk away, but before leaving, he turned and asked, "Do you wanna hit the road or wait for the medical examiner?"

"I'll stay," Nick replied weakly.

"Okay," Florski said, patting Nick's shoulder once more before turning and walking toward a group of EMTs huddled near their ambulance.

The new kid was going to be okay.

—CHAPTER 16—

DEADLY FORCE
"I Fought the Law" (Bryan Adams)

When Chimlyn showed up, everything was the way he thought it should be. The gate was locked, but he could gain entrance by swerving around the same large boulders he'd avoided with Bobber Wangsness back in their high school days when they used to throw rocks as high as they could, then admire the disgusting plop as the stones disappeared into the thick, putrid muck. The good old shit pits, a place to be avoided—or to bury bad police chiefs.

He parked the car, turned off the lights, grabbed his shovel, and started to dig. His first thought was to dig the grave six feet deep, but he quickly realized that was easier said than done. It was almost impossible to keep the fetid ooze from running back into the hole as quickly as he could shovel it out. After a few minutes, he heard the sound of sirens to the east. Were they coming for him? He stopped digging and listened closely.

He had thought he heard a crashing noise as he was stepping out of the car, as well as a long, loud train whistle. To the east, he could see a glow in the night sky, and though he had no idea what was going on, he was too busy to worry about it at the moment. There was still work left to be done.

He began digging again, then decided that a hole four feet deep was deep enough. After all, Badge wasn't going to climb out, but Chimlyn had to, and he realized that it wasn't going to be easy. Any indecision was cleared up when he suddenly hit solid rock and could dig no deeper. He had no choice—it was as deep as Badge was going to go.

Chimlyn finally was able to crawl out of the hole after digging several foot holes in the side of the grave. As his chest heaved while he was trying to catch his breath, Chimlyn wiped the stinging sweat from his eyes. He was very glad the long day would be over soon.

He opened the trunk and wrestled the tarp-wrapped cadaver out, then half dragged and half carried it to the hole. He rolled it into the opening and it fell to the bottom of the pit with a dull thud. He then tossed everything else from the trunk on top of the body.

He really wanted to toss the crossbow and arrows into the hole, too, but he decided to stick to his plan. It would be best to keep that stuff away from the body. The first shovel loads of dirt made a rattling nose as they thudded onto the tarp. Excess dirt started piling up after the hole was full, but he spread it around the area, even covering the freshly disturbed dirt with dead cattails and leaves. He tossed the shovel into the trunk, found a rock, put it into the sack with the crossbow, and tossed them onto the passenger side floor where he could get to them quickly when he found a good place to toss them.

It had been a long day, and it was so good to know he was finally headed home to his bed. He had worked hard to finish the worst day of his life, and he was exhausted.

Then, as he opened the car door, he decided that he should probably say a prayer for Badge. Chimlyn wanted to be a good Christian even more than he wanted Badge out of his marriage, so he improvised a quick prayer.

"We thank the Lord for happy hearts and rain and sunny weather. For the graves we dig—and that he's gone forever."

It was a good prayer and Chimlyn was satisfied with it. Badge wouldn't be hurting any more families. Chimlyn had executed a perfect plan—but his luck was about to change. All the hard stuff was done. Now all he had to do was get rid of the arrows. If Robin was home when he got back, that would be great, though he was too tired to hash things over.

As he drove along the gravel road back to town, he discovered that a train was blocking the road. He hated when trains stopped for no apparent reason and blocked roads for a long time.

He saw lights flashing on the other side of the tracks, and as he got closer, he could see that the glow was coming from spotlights on squad cars. A train must have hit a car, he decided, which would explain all the sirens he had heard earlier.

Any other time he would have stopped to see what was happening, but he was just too tired. He knew the whole town would be talking about it the next day, so he wouldn't miss anything. He'd find out everything soon enough.

Chief Fellows had responded to the scene as requested by the deputies. After they'd run the plates and found identification in a purse, they'd asked Frankie to come, wanting to give him the information in person so he could relay it to the family.

"Yeah, Chief, she's dead," said one of the officers. "That pretty little thing who used to work at the Ben Franklin. It's real bad, let me tell you."

"Are you sure?" Frankie asked. "I don't want to go getting folks riled up for nothing!"

"We're sure," the officer said. "We'll have her taken to the funeral home. Let us know which one."

Fellows clenched his teeth, sighed, then said, "I'll get right on it. Jesus Christ, I hate this part of the job. It never gets any easier!"

It was a Friday night and Frankie mulled over what to say as he got into his squad car. He had to tell Robin's parents the horrible news. He also needed to persuade them to stay away from the scene. Having a grief-stricken family show up at the scene of a fatality only made things worse.

Then Chief Fellows remembered that he'd seen Robin's husband at the Kwik Trip earlier that night. He needed to be notified, too. In fact, it would be easier for the chief to tell Chimlyn and then let him tell the rest of the family that Robin was dead.

Just as he fired up the engine, the chief saw Chimlyn's vehicle disappearing down the road, headed for town after crossing the tracks at the next open crossing. It made sense. Robin had probably been going to meet him before she was killed. He pulled out and sped toward town to catch up with Chimlyn.

As he got close to Chimlyn's yellow Plymouth, the chief turned on his car's overheads, but instead of stopping, Chimlyn sped up. The situation had escalated from a death notification to a high speed chase.

Chimlyn panicked when he saw the police lights behind him. He was in a fight-or-flight situation, and he chose flight. Although he knew the back roads as well as anybody, he was unable to shake Chief Fellows. As they drove, Frankie got on the radio to report the chase to dispatch.

"This is Chief Fellows. I'm in pursuit of a yellow Plymouth Road Runner, believed driven by Chimlyn Johnson. We're heading toward Madelia on Plover Crossing Road. I don't know if this has to do with his wife getting killed tonight, but I'm going to continue the pursuit and find out."

Many people in town had police scanners and heard about the chase, but one person was especially shocked at the news. Robin's mom was doing the dishes and had turned the scanner on when she heard the sirens. Now she had just heard that it was Robin who had been killed and that the chief was chasing Chimlyn down the road.

Robin's mom shrieked with anguish, and when her husband rushed into the kitchen to see what was going on, she slumped into a chair and sobbed, "Our baby's dead."

At that moment, Chimlyn was unknowingly heading straight toward a state trooper who had been responding to the accident when he heard the chief's report. He got on the radio and contacted Chief Fellows, identifying himself as Trooper Rhodes and offering his assistance.

The chief responded, "Fellows to Rhodes. No known reason for chase. What's your 10-20?"

"Rhodes to Fellows, I'm a half a mile east of you. I'll slow him down with stop sticks before he hits town."

"Acknowledge that, over," Fellows responded.

Chimlyn's panic was growing stronger as he failed to shake the red lights in his rearview mirror. In his terrified state, he shouted to himself, "Maybe the cops know all about it and that's why they're chasing me. I got caught up in some bad stuff and now everyone's going to hate me."

There was no other choice. He had to keep running. He just couldn't get caught!

As he rounded a turn, he saw a state patrol car blocking the road, its red lights flashing. Chimlyn decided to hit the brakes and bail out of the car. At least then he could throw the arrows away. The tires smoked as Chimlyn's car screeched to a halt. Chimlyn leaned over and grabbed the arrows, then jumped out of the car and sprinted toward an open field.

As Chief Fellows pulled in behind the Plymouth, he could see that Chimlyn was carrying something in his right hand. Was it a gun? As Chimlyn raised his hand to throw away the arrows, Chief Fellows emerged from the squad car and fired three shots in rapid succession. A moment later, he was hurrying to join Trooper Rhodes as he approached Chimlyn's body lying in the road.

Chimlyn looked up, but his mind was all confused. He wanted to keep hearing, but his ears were beginning to fail. Sounds were still coming in, but he couldn't make sense of them. It was like trying to tune in a distant radio station. Everything was being drowned out by static. A black spot took the place of what he'd been seeing and started to swell until everything became dark and quiet. He found himself drifting into a suffocating foggy place. Everything—time, concerns, memories, and even his love for Robin—slowly yielded to nothingness as he slipped into the cold finality of death.

Nothing can stand in the way of death, and when it arrives, it settles its accounts with everyone. Chimlyn's accounts had been settled—paid with the only currency death will accept—his life. Chimlyn Johnson became just another memory in people's minds, never to be a living factor again.

As Chief Fellows approached, Trooper Rhodes looked at him curiously, but said nothing. Instead, he shone his flashlight on the arrows Chimlyn still clutched in his right hand.

"What was he going to do with those, throw 'em at us?" Rhodes asked. When the chief didn't respond, he added, "Looks like the medical examiner is gonna be busy tonight, huh?"

Reaching down, Trooper Rhodes picked up something shiny from next to Chimlyn's body. "This must have fallen out of his pocket. It looks brand new."

Frankie took the badge and examined it. It was a chief of police badge from the town of Normal.

"Chief, are you with me?" Rhodes asked.

Frankie just shook his head and mumbled, "Christ, his wife is dead back on the railroad tracks, and now I killed him—just because of some arrows."

"Come on, Chief," said Rhodes. "You had no choice. Pull yourself together."

As Frankie stood over Chimlyn's body, Rhodes called dispatch to report that the chase had ended. A short time later, other officers arrived, set up crime scene tape, and took statements.

Chief Fellows would later be cleared of any wrongdoing, but he would carry the guilt with him the rest of his life. He had killed a kid whose family had always let him hunt on their farm—a kid who didn't even have a gun. Chief Fellows would spend the rest of his life trying to wash away his guilt with alcohol.

After the shooting, the Johnson family made a homemade memorial with a white cross and plastic flowers and a picture of Chimlyn smiling with his arm around Robin stapled to the cross inside a plastic sandwich bag. Fellows made it a point to avoid that stretch of road from that day on.

He also tried to avoid seeing any member of the Johnson family, which wasn't easy in a small town. One day, Chimlyn's dad ran into the chief outside of the grocery store.

"Chief," Mr. Johnson said, "You're still welcome to hunt on our land. I saw a fine buck in the back forty the other day. If you want, I'll hold off so you can get the first crack at him."

As the two men shook hands, tears rolled down Frankie's cheeks. He wept even harder still when Mr. Johnson enfolded him in a warm embrace. He hadn't been able to escape in the bottle, but feeling Mr.

Johnson's forgiveness offered him the freedom he had been desperately seeking for so long.

After Mr. Johnson had left, Frankie Fellows drove slowly out to Plover Road and approached the memorial he'd never seen but knew full well was there. He stood and stared at the name as the sun slid down toward the horizon: CHIMLYN MARK JOHNSON.

He sank to his knees in front of the homemade cross and sobbed, "Oh, Chimlyn, I'm so sorry. So sorry. You were a great kid. You were never any trouble. Was there a reason for what happened? I'll never know, but I just want you to know how sorry I am."

One flew east . . .

—CHAPTER 17—

SASSY/AGNES
"The End" (The Doors)

If you didn't count television friends, her home life was spent in solitary confinement. Nobody called. Nobody stopped by. Occasionally the phone rang and she'd hear a caller leave a message. Usually it involved great deals on life insurance or residential siding.

She had long since given up trying to make it to the phone before the answering machine kicked in. Her knees burned, her hip throbbed, and her guts always seemed to be on fire. She couldn't crawl out of bed without being slapped in the face by a new physical calamity.

The bad stomach had been with her for as long as she could remember. The hip thing made it hard to sit in her chair but if she laid down she couldn't get up without Badge's help, but he had always been so self-centered. He was away from home more than not.

She was also irate because she had to stagger into the kitchen to scrounge up her own food. Luckily, her two best friends never left the

165

house—the fridge and her beloved TV. She loved them almost as much as Badge loved his computer.

Her routine consisted of dragging plenty of treats into the living room to munch on while watching her favorite shows. The news networks irritated her more, especially when they started whining about how cops were screwing up cases. She was embarrassed for her husband.

Badge was going to be out of town on the day before Halloween. He'd asked her to go, but she had refused. When he left, he had promised to be home all day on Halloween. She decided that if he didn't keep his promise this time, there would be hell to pay.

Agnes had one more problem to dwell on. For the past week she had started producing methane, which was strange, because she hadn't changed her diet or anything. She was confused by her latest calamity, but all she could do at the moment was pray that her flatulence storm would eventually blow itself out.

In the kitchen, decision making could be distressing for Agnes at times. Brownies, cheesy hot dish, and pizza never failed to transport her back to happier times spent behind closed doors with mommy. She could eat and be safe from the other kids and their nasty taunting. A full stomach always provided relief from an empty life.

Her decision that day was to attack a cold pizza and wash it down with a half gallon of milk. She didn't even make it out of the kitchen before demolishing the pizza, but she eventually flopped into her recliner with a pan of brownies, a bag of cookies, and another half gallon of whole milk.

The brownies were consumed with maximum restraint in an effort to make them last as long as possible. She stared at the TV, not seeing it, her thoughts centered on her idiot husband.

"If you had half the brains god gave a goose, my tummy wouldn't bother me," she thought. "And if I was being seen by a competent physician in a bigger town, I'd be cured already and wouldn't have to suffer like this. There has to be a cure for my condition!"

A large city hospital with competent doctors was what she needed. If she could just get the burning to go away in her knees, she could finally lay her hands on the glass plates that would force others to give her the acknowledgment she deserved. The people of Minnesota would love her for it. The governor might even recognize her.

Those thoughts exhilarated her. It was a relief to have something to dwell on other than her husband. The last time they'd been to Madelia, both the Pullets had returned home in excellent spirits. Agnes had been around one of her life's great loves, and Badge had indulged his own passion.

Agnes thought back to her own family life, which had always been prim and proper. Her mother and father never tolerated anything but the most courteous behavior. No one was allowed to be rude or obnoxious. Agnes found serenity in the order and decorum, though she was burned by the laughter and cruel comments of the kids at school.

Her thoughts then turned to her marriage. How she ended up married, she'd never know. While at Cecil's having a nice respectable dinner one night, she had somehow ended up getting engaged. On the day of the wedding, she remembered how the merrymakers tapped their glasses with their spoons to prompt the couple to kiss. It had felt so wrong and icky, and she didn't want to do, it, but felt like she had to.

It wasn't until their honeymoon at Mackinac Island that the stomachaches began. Then her weight began to creep up, but she handled the problem by avoiding the scale.

Her local doctor had tried to tell her how detrimental her weight gain was, encouraging her to take control of the situation and change her lifestyle, but Agnes ignored his advice. After all, he wasn't able to diagnose why her stomach hurt all the time, so why should she listen to anything he had to say? Agnes had turned and indignantly stormed out of the doctor's office, aided to the car by a thoroughly embarrassed Badge.

Agnes had always been a clean person, but it was hard to get everything properly clean without a shower. She had even taken to wearing perfume, and though it never prompted the type of romantic scenes she saw on commercials, it did make her feel prettier.

Conversations between Badge and Agnes never strayed away from police work. Lately they had centered on McMurphy and Badge's efforts to get rid of him, though Badge had once complemented her on how nice she smelled—but only once.

While Badge had become an important chief of police, Agnes had fallen into a cold, dark, lonely, place. As she got bigger, her world got smaller. He never seemed to have any desire to make her happy, except for bringing her pizza, and everything he did seemed to piss her off— yet she lived in constant fear of losing him.

That afternoon her fears overrode her inaction. She struggled into the bathroom, put her hair up, put on perfume, and made his favorite supper—tater tot hot dish. She had everything in its proper place— except her insecurities—but she wanted to change and had finally done something about it. She'd keep the hot dish warm, since he had told her he was going to be late.

But Badge never came home.

After waiting until way past bedtime, Agnes called the station, but Badge didn't answer the phone. Had he lied to her again? She was furious and terrified as she stared at the television, munching on popcorn and a gallon of ice cream.

It took a lot of effort to pull herself up to her feet after her snack. Then she tottered to the bedroom and fell into bed, but she couldn't sleep. Sometime during the night, around two or three, she got up for some more cupcakes and milk to ease her churning stomach.

As she was lying wide awake in bed again, the phone rang. It was the station calling.

"Yes, Mrs. Pullet, I'm sorry to wake you, but is the chief home?"

"No, he's not, but can I help you?"

"Well, Mrs. Pullet, the chief's car was found in the Oakwood Cemetery, and we've been notified by the authorities in Madelia that a man was picked up in possession of the chief's badge. Would you be willing to speak to an investigator about this?"

"Of course," Agnes said. "I'll get dressed and be ready by the time someone gets here."

Her mind was reeling from the news. There were so many possibilities, but all of them led back to the same conclusion: something was very wrong. The more she thought about it, the more wrong it felt.

After getting dressed, she sat by the door and waited for the investigator. She wondered what Badge would have wanted her to say. He had so carefully constructed his entire life behind a curtain of lies. Maybe he had run away with that woman, and she herself had been the victim of her husband's latest lie. The thought was almost too much to bear. What would she do without him?

When the investigator arrived, he told Agnes what they had learned to that point. They knew that Badge's car had been found in the cemetery. They knew that his badge had been found in the pocket of a man by the name of Chimlyn Johnson who had been shot and killed in Madelia after a high-speed car chase.

"Have you ever heard of Chimlyn Johnson?" asked the inspector. "It's kind of an unusual name. Did you ever hear the chief mention that name?"

"No," Agnes lied, shaking her head, "and Badge would never give his badge away. We both know that."

"Johnson had a wife," the inspector continued. "Her name was… let me look…Robin. She was from Madelia. Was your husband there recently? Oh, and something else that's strange. Robin was killed by a train last night, so she and her husband both died on the same night. When the police ordered the husband to stop after he vacated the vehicle, he kept running and they shot him—but when they looked in his hand, he was holding some arrows and he had Badge's badge in his pocket. I gotta tell you, I can't make heads or tails out of it, and now the chief is missing."

Something about the name of the town struck a chord with Agnes. "Wasn't there just a convention in Mankato?" she asked.

"No, ma'am," replied the investigator. "Mankato was last year. This year it's going to be up in St. Cloud."

"It's in St. Cloud?" Agnes asked, her eyes narrowing.

Now she knew. Her lying husband had been up to his old tricks. Maybe he had been with Robin and had left his badge on the nightstand, where her husband had found it and stuck it in his pocket.

Noticing Agnes's change in attitude and demeanor, the investigator asked, "Why'd you think there was a convention in Mankato, ma'am?"

"Oh, I don't know," she said, "I'm just upset and confused, I guess."

The investigator assured her he'd stay in touch and then asked her to call him if she heard anything, but Agnes barely heard his words. Her mind was focused on how her life was about to change.

"Oh, one more thing," the investigator asked before he left. "They found some glass plate pictures of the state capitol in Badges' trunk. Would you have any idea what that would be about?"

Agnes gasped, then quickly collected herself, shrugged, and said, "I'm sure they're nothing. How important could pictures of an old government building be, after all?"

The investigator left Agnes to wrestle with thoughts and fears. She went into the kitchen, made two sandwiches, and downed them with a carton of milk. She ate mechanically. She was only going through the motions and eating offered no consolation. She was tired and her mind was drifting without clinging to anything.

Then she thought about Martin McMurphy.

On the rich side of the tracks, where Mr. and Mrs. Gotrocks lived, misery had settled into Junior's life. No matter how much he tried to pretend, Sassy always took time to explain the reality of things. His accomplishments, whether big or small, were always ignored.

Sassy remained a one woman male-wrecking machine. Junior could never undo the words and actions of an alcoholic father. He was left to wallow in the aftermath of a scorned daughter's wrath about anything to do with men while Sassy worked tirelessly to escape her father's slurred words and beery breath.

Superintendent Beane was feared for good reason by all district employees. Men had made it so easy for Sassy. None of them had any back-bone—just limp dicks, the way she saw it. They could be lied to, threatened, or screwed into their place. Her life was so easy that it was almost boring.

Junior had somehow managed to live under the sweltering heat of her scorn, knowing he was tolerated, at best. Their children had each been conceived during an intoxicated night of coitus—at least that's what Junior thought. Red wine helped silence her daddy's words while she was being entered—and Sassy found no challenge in getting him to mount her. She could have Junior any time she wanted. All it took was a simple drop of her panties.

Sassy would wake up to each new better day and immediately start seething her way back to her twisted state of being. No flowers would grow in the garden their marriage had become. Co-workers, family, and pretend friends started avoiding them. They were just too uncomfortable to be around.

Sassy was aware of how important her school district was for her and she couldn't do anything that would jeopardize her position. She loved lording over her minions more than she loved breathing. The district was populated with people who were happier than she was, and she considered it her sacred duty to make them pay for everything they had that she didn't. She prided herself on the knowledge that she could make any employee in her district suffer. Everyone in her life seemed miserable except Junior, and she was sure that in good time she'd figure out how to give him the pain and suffering he deserved.

The pleasure of causing pain actually became a sexual stimulant. While waiting in her office for the arrival of a summoned employee, she found her nipples became sensitive and she experienced dampness between her legs. She loved the feeling and it started replacing any need she'd ever had for Knucklehead, as she called Junior.

Somehow Knucklehead appeared to deflect the pain, making him the only real failure in her life. His manhood disgusted her, his stupidity annoyed her, but he had done her an even bigger wrong by fathering rejects that embarrassed her. How could he possibly be one-upping her? He was too stupid to be a match for her, and it gnawed at her and drove her to start downing several more glasses of wine than she needed at the end of the evenings.

Sassy had actually been excited about the arrival of her children. She had been smug with the realization that she'd be delivering perfect babies, and she'd provide them with everything they needed—everything she'd been denied when she was growing up.

She had wanted to mother homecoming queens and gridiron heroes, smart, sexy and athletic. With the money she made, they'd never have to struggle like she'd had to do, and she'd make sure they had braces if they needed them.

When her first daughter arrived, she looked too much like Sassy to be considered beautiful, and though Sassy never admitted that she wasn't exactly Miss America, she was passable. Then the rest of her five children started arriving. Sassy noted that her last four children had a bottom lip that hung down and seemed listless and dull. The other students were nice to them, but they were never among the popular kids in school.

"Even if my kids were treated like shit, they'd be too damn dumb to know. They get that from Knucklehead, and he's going to pay dearly for that!" Sassy found herself growling into the bottom of an empty wine glass.

She made promises to try and make it to their games and concerts, but after a while, she started making sure she was too busy. The pain of their ineptitude was just too much. When the children started having difficulty with their homework, Sassy tried tutors, the Sylvan Center, and even slapping the drool off their faces, but nothing helped.

Junior tried his best, but he never found the right words to talk the tears away from his children's eyes after they had suffered Sassy's verbal humiliation. She never realized that she was doing to her own children just what her despised father had done to her as she wallowed in her silent world of hatred and self-loathing.

Tormenting school employees by day and drinking her wine at night got her through each day, but she never could shake her feeling of hopelessness and desperation at home. She pushed Junior in directions he didn't want to go, but she was too wrapped up in herself to notice or to care. For his part, Junior lived behind a carefully constructed façade of the caring husband. Ironically, if Sassy had ever known how much pain she was truly causing him she would have been delighted.

After arriving at the club for lunch one day, Sassy found that no amount of red wine could erase Knucklehead's odor, bad breath, and stupidity. From the very beginning of the evening, she began firing arrows of contempt at the husband she wanted to hurt so badly—and suddenly Junior began to feel the pain in a whole new way.

As they left the club and headed for the interstate, Sassy was at the wheel, because being in control was imperative. "Come on," she goaded, "wouldn't you like to see your loving wifey with another man? You could babysit while we were doing it!"

"Please don't be mean today," Junior said sullenly. "Let's go to Applebee's. The first round's on me. You whine, I whine, we all whine for red wine," he added in a feeble attempt at levity.

Looking at her husband with contempt, Sassy added, "You know, I think I'd like to experience a man with twice the junk you got. I wanna pull into the fuck station and say fill 'er up! Is that too much to ask? I'm still young and pretty—and I want someone besides you!"

Before Junior could say anything (if indeed he had intended to), she moaned with mock passion, "Oh, Badge, take me!" She looked over to gauge the effect and continued, "Oh, Badge, make me scream like Knucklehead never could. Make me your little loosey goosey."

Struggling to stay under control, Junior went back to the ditty the guys used to sing when he was in college. "Come on, Sassy, sing with me. You whine, I whine, we all whine for red wine."

Ignoring her pleading husband, Sassy began to chant, "I want Badge! I want Badge!"

But even as she chanted, she knew that it was Martin McMurphy that was causing her to get moist between her legs. He was the one man who had put her in her place, and it caused an aching in her loins, but since her mind wanted to hate him, the tingling of her clitoris confused her. Then she did something crueler than anything she'd ever done to Junior before.

Looking directly into his eyes, she said, "I need to make a confession. Badge screwed me, Mr. Junior. Can you ever forgive me?" Then she laughed and added, "And he's so much bigger than you that you wouldn't believe it. Would you like to hide in the closet so you can see how a real man puts the wood to his slut? It makes me hot all over just thinking about it."

Seeing the look of pain that Junior was trying desperately to hid,

Sassy knew she was finally exacting her revenge. She was finally getting to him! Then something unexpected happened.

Sassy's tongue slipped as she continued to taunt her husband. "Oh, Martin—I mean Badge—I can't wait for you to put it in me again, and this time we'll let Junior watch so he can learn something."

Even Sassy was surprised to hear Martin's name pop out in the middle of her lurid tirade, but Junior's mind was in utter turmoil. He had always suspected her of infidelity, but she had just admitted it point-blank—and then told him she was going to keep doing it! The thing he wasn't sure of was if it was with Badge or Martin McMurphy. Maybe it was with both of them—with Sassy, anything was possible.

Inexplicably, Sassy grew quiet. She had been delivering a serious of crushing blows, but had suddenly lapsed into silence. Junior was upset, but he maintained his docile façade, making the silence in the car even more deafening.

He had always been able to ignore her ramblings. He had always harbored the hope that things would get better. But at that moment something inside of Junior snapped. Maybe Sassy had figured he was too slow to catch her verbal slip, but she had figured wrong. She had spent their entire married life trying to hurt him to the quick—and she had just succeeded.

He had always held firmly to an ideal image of what a marriage should be. He had always dreamed that his life would be filled with friends and family. He had always longed to have healthy, happy children. He had always wished for a loving wife like the other wives he saw at the club, smiling, laughing, and holding hands with their husbands.

But he had never gotten any of those things, and now it was time for some payback. He knew he had to do something, and for the first time, he was prepared to do it.

One flew west…

—CHAPTER 18—

AGNES/SASSY
"Dyin'" (Trampled by Turtles)

Junior was just getting in his car and pulling out of his driveway, on his way to pick two Irish clients up at the Rochester airport on a cold late-October Halloween afternoon. He envisioned himself in a boat, half frozen with drunken Irishmen clients while Sassy was supposed to be at home alone. He didn't like the idea of being in northern Minnesota while his wife was running around with the police chief.

He also wondered how Martin McMurphy fit into the picture. He was sick and tired of his life and wanted to make some changes—and he'd start with his wife. He'd show her what kind of man he was. Was she getting it someplace else, being serviced by two cops?

There was a time when she had let him have at her when she was dead drunk, but even that had stopped. Her legs were always crossed. Something was wrong with his marriage, and he had to fight to make it right.

He was going to be stuck with a pair of drunken Irish clients, making it easy for Sassy to get what she was looking for with him out of town. Absent-mindedly, he heard a reporter on the radio babbling about a girl who'd been hit by a train and killed in Madelia. And then, to make it worse, the cops had shot her husband.

"Just like cops to kill a poor distraught bastard the same day he lost his wife," Junior thought. "Well, as of today, I'm gonna start dealing with some cops myself."

He looked into the rearview mirror and saw nets, poles, and tackle boxes full of fishing gear. He was a good company man, but he liked to think he was an even better family man. He had dutifully given Sassy a goodbye peck when he left, but she had just mumbled something without even opening her blue eyes.

Now he was headed to a huge northern lake in the middle of a huge forest—in the middle of his empty life. Their marriage was a contaminated mess of icy words and cold actions. Sassy had wanted to get back at her daddy, but his early death had robbed her of the pleasure of showing him how much she hated him—and she had never let Junior have a moment's peace because of it.

All he wanted was a happy wife, happy kids, and a happy life—but that's not what he had gotten. No one in the Beane household was happy, and now his wife was bedding police officers instead of him, and it had to end. He wasn't sure how to do it, but it had to end.

Suddenly, he took a left on a street that he knew would lead him toward Badge's house. When he pulled up to the curb, he was surprised at how small the house was. It wouldn't have made a suitable doghouse on the property he owned.

Although he didn't have a real plan, he stepped out of the car, walked up to the front door, and rang the doorbell. If nothing else, he wasn't going to sneak around like Badge did with married women like

Sassy. He'd knock, address the situation head-on, then continue to the airport with a clear conscience. One thing he wouldn't do was allow himself to be dragged down to Badge's level. For once in his miserable life, he was going to stand tall.

After waiting just long enough to decide that no one was home, Junior startled when an enormous woman answered the door leaning heavily on a black cane.

She stared at him for a moment, then asked, "Yes? May I be of some assistance?"

Junior's mind went temporarily blank. Then he gathered his wits and said, "Yes, ma'am. Is Chief Pullet home? I'd like to talk to him about something important. He does live here, right?"

"Yes, he does," said Agnes, "but the chief isn't home at the moment. Is there something I can help you with?"

"No, ma'am," Junior said, shaking his head. "I'd like to talk to the chief in private. Do you know when the best time to talk to him would be? I'll be out of town for a few days, but I can come back whenever it's convenient for him."

When Agnes hesitated, Junior suddenly decided to take a new tack. Taking a deep breath, he blurted out, "Look, Mrs. Pullet, My name is Junior Beane, and I have reason to believe that your husband has been sleeping with my…my wife…and I'd like it to stop!"

Only after he had finished his speech did he breathe again. To his amazement, Agnes didn't flinch, gasp, or show any sign of emotion at all. Then, just as he was deciding that he had shocked her so much that she was unable to speak, Agnes's face began to pale noticeably and her eyes filled with tears.

"I'm sorry, ma'am," Junior said. "I know it's a shock, but I just found out myself, and it was a shock to me, too."

Wiping a tear from her cheek, Agnes asked softly, "May I ask you, Mr. Beane, is your wife nicknamed Phoebe? Do you know a man named Chimlyn? Do you know how long my husband has been seeing your wife?"

Now that it was all out in the open, Junior and Agnes stood and talked for as long as Agnes was able to stand. They stood on the front porch and talked quietly for several excruciating minutes until Junior looked at his watch and told her he needed to get to the airport.

As he drove away, Junior was filled with conflicting emotions. He was proud of himself for taking action, but he felt so sorry for the huge woman who obviously was only now learning the full extent of her husband's cheating. He had finally shown Sassy that he was a man—a real man—even though he had just sent Badge's wife's world crumbling to the ground.

But he couldn't worry about Badge's wife. His own life was worth fighting for. He pondered how he would let Sassy know that he had confronted one of her lovers. He no longer dreaded the upcoming fishing trip, knowing Agnes would be having it out with Badge the next time she saw him. At least one of the cops was out of Sassy's life. He'd deal with the other one when he got back from northern Minnesota.

Junior's visit had been both unexpected but to be expected at the same time. She wasn't really surprised to hear that Badge had been involved with still another woman. She could only wonder how many others there had been, and how long it had been going on. She actually admired the courage it had taken for Junior to show up at their front door.

She'd probably never see Badge again, and for the first time since the ordeal had begun, she really didn't care. For some reason, her thoughts were fixated on Martin McMurphy. There was no one she could call to talk about her pain. She was running on empty and somehow, thought she couldn't explain why, she began to believe that only Martin McMurphy could help.

Agnes had arrived at the darkest place a human being can go—the place where all hope disappears. Her mind began to drift to the thought of ending it all. There was a bottle of Oxycontin and a liter of vodka in the house. That would do it. She could slit her wrists, but she didn't really know how to do it. She couldn't hang herself. She was just too heavy. She could drive her car into a bridge abutment. She couldn't shoot herself. Badge had taken away the gun.

Even as she wallowed in delicious thoughts of killing herself, Agnes began to feel more anger than remorse. Damn it! She was a person and she deserved better than what she was getting!

Then her thoughts turned back to Martin McMurphy. He was always laughing and enjoying himself. He made fun of proper etiquette and polite behavior—two things that had always been central to her life. He probably didn't even go to church, although Agnes herself had been forced to stop going when she could no longer fit into a pew.

"He's always pawing that skinny wife of his," Agnes thought. "If Lacy had the health problems I have, she wouldn't be so skinny."

Agnes then turned and wobbled into the kitchen, where she picked up her car keys and cell phone. She slipped the phone into her pocket and after a quick bite to settle her stomach, she headed for the garage. She was on a mission. She had failed to get the job done the last time, but she wasn't going to fail again—and she'd be killing two birds with one stone. It was a good plan.

She drove toward the mall parking ramp. Pulling out her cell phone, she dialed Martin McMurphy's number.

"Hello?"

"Is that you, Martin?" Agnes said.

Pausing, Martin said reluctantly, "Agnes? Why are you calling me, of all people?"

"We have to talk," Agnes said, ignoring Martin's question. "I know something about the drug charges, but I need to meet you in the mall parking ramp. Do you still drive that little red sports car?"

When Martin said yes, Agnes added, "Maybe you'll want to bring Lacy with you. I'm sure she'll also be pleased to hear what I'm going to tell you."

Martin hesitated, trying to figure out what was going on. First he'd gotten a strange phone call from that guy in Madelia, and then an equally mysterious call from Badge's wife. Finally, he agreed to meet Agnes at the designated place.

Agnes arrived first and waited at the top of the ramp, watching the street below for Martin's car to appear. What a surprise she had in store for him!

When she saw the red sports car come into view, she stepped to the edge of the building and hurled herself into the empty space below, hoping she had timed it so she would land right in front of Martin McMurphy and his skinny wife. The last laugh would be hers!

Unfortunately for Agnes, she wasn't able to see the horrified expression on Martin McMurphy's face as he swerved to a stop after she had slammed into the hood and windshield of his car. She also would never know that Martin had come alone, so his skinny wife never saw the gruesome mess she had created.

As Martin leaped from the car, his mind in overdrive, but he was startled back to reality by a woman screaming that she had called 911. Staring at the dead woman, he finally realized who it was.

He stood as a crowd began to gather, but he didn't let on that he knew anything about what had happened. He wasn't a cop anymore—Agnes's husband had seen to that—so he found himself acting like any other witness to a horrific accident.

As Junior headed toward Rochester, he felt good—better than he'd felt in years. The fishing trip with the Irishmen wasn't going to be bad, after all. He was actually looking forward to it. He had taken care of the first part of his marital problems, and he had every intention of taking care of the rest of them when he returned home. He even decided to call Sassy on his cell phone.

"Yeah, Junior. What do you want?" Sassy asked indifferently.

"I thought I'd tell you that I went to Badge Pullet's house to call him out."

"You what?" Sassy said in disbelief.

"You heard me," Junior said firmly. "He wasn't there, but I had a long talk with his wife while I was there."

Sassy listened in stunned silence. Could the voice on the other end of the phone really be the mealy-mouthed nobody she had been married to for so many miserable years?

She waited till Junior was done talking, then said, "Look, Junior. Do you really think I'd waste my time on a guy like Badge Pullet? Christ, even you've got more balls than Badge!" But being the cruel person she was, she felt compelled to add, "Maybe Martin McMurphy, but not that sorry-ass wimp, Badge Pullet."

When the phone line went dead, Sassy didn't know if Junior had hung up or if the call had been dropped. On Junior's end, however, he knew that the phone had fallen to the floor after her cruel remark. He had gone from being a superman to a whiny little brat in a heartbeat.

As Junior drove past the mall, he saw several people gathered around a small red sports car. He recognized the car—and then he saw Martin McMurphy and something snapped inside his brain. He wrapped his fingers tightly around the steering wheel and clenched his teeth, Sassy's taunting words echoing through his mind.

Martin McMurphy's attention was focused on the mangled lump of flesh on the road and didn't even see Junior's car coming as it plowed into him with a huge thud, instantly breaking both of his legs and sending him soaring into the air.

Not content with simply breaking Martin's legs, Junior leapt from the SUV, opened the back door, and rummaged through the tackle boxes until he found a razor sharp filleting knife. Then he pulled it out and rushed toward Martin's motionless body.

Struggling to breathe after the impact, Martin found himself staring up toward the sky. Then Junior Beane's face appeared above him, a wild and malevolent look in his eyes. Junior raised the knife high into the air, then plunged it into Martin's stomach. Backed by Junior's full weight, the blade slid completely through Martin's body and didn't stop until it scraped against the cement below.

As the bystanders screamed and ran for cover, Martin's blood spurted onto the sidewalk, mingling with Agnes's. Death had punched his ticket to eternity as he clung to his last thoughts of Lacy. Only when Martin had finally breathed his last gasp did Junior twist the blade back out, lean back, and smile as the wail of approaching sirens started to echo through the streets.

And one flew over...

—CHAPTER 19—

LACY
"When Doves Cry" (Prince)

It was a typical cold damp night in Minnesota. Folks had to bundle up if they were going to venture outside.

"It's cold outside. Put on your minks, let's ride," kids in Normal sang as they put on their Halloween costumes, excited about the prospect of loading up on candy. They had waited weeks to dress up and haunt their neighborhoods.

They'd been told by their parents that monsters weren't real, but there was no way anyone could have known that a real monster had dressed up like a police chief in their own town of Normal. He had spent years masquerading as a hero of the community while spewing nastiness onto married women, but he had finally gotten caught in the web of deceit he spun.

Lacy hurried home after work that night. She didn't want to miss the trick-or-treaters. She loved kids and she loved teaching because it gave her a chance to spend entire days with them.

As she pulled up to the house, she saw that Martin's car was gone. That was strange, since he loved to help her interact with the costumed children on Halloween night.

When she entered the kitchen, she saw a note pinned to the refrigerator with a magnet. It read: "Had to run. Agnes Pullet called and needs to talk. Should be home before you, but if not, don't eat all the Snickers!"

Lacy was surprised and perplexed. Why would Agnes Pullet have called Martin to talk, of all people? It didn't make sense.

Her thoughts were interrupted by a knock on the front door. Lacy opened the door and got another surprise. It was Lieutenant Gloomy Statements of the Normal police department. Lacy instantly sensed that something was wrong.

"Lieutenant," she said, "please come in."

The lieutenant didn't move. Instead, he said in a formal tone, "Mrs. McMurphy, I regret to inform you that your husband lost his life tonight in an accident."

"No!" Lacy shrieked. "He was only going to meet—"

The lieutenant interrupted, "I'm afraid it's true, Mrs. McMurphy. Your husband was taken to the hospital, but he died on the way."

There was a long, uncomfortable silence, after which Lacy asked again, "Will you please come in and tell me everything you know, lieutenant?"

The lieutenant refused anything to drink as he sat, stiff and formal, on a couch in the living room. "H—how did it happen?" Lacy asked, her voice barely above a whisper. "I—I just don't understand. He wasn't on police business."

"He hit," the lieutenant began, then hesitated, as if trying to find a way to tell the strange story in a way that would make any sense. "He swerved to avoid hitting Agnes Pullet, who had jumped off the top story of the parking ramp. Then, after getting out of his car, a man named Junior Beane—Superintendent Beane's husband—showed up at the scene and stabbed him."

"Stabbed him? Why?" Lacy gasped.

"Apparently Agnes had wanted Martin to hit her and tried to time her jump so she'd land in front of his car," the lieutenant said. "We don't quite know the motive yet, but that's what we're guessing as of this moment."

"She set him up?" Lacy asked softly.

"Not yet," replied the lieutenant. "No one seems to know where the chief is, although his abandoned car was found in a cemetery and his badge was found in the pocket of a man who had been shot in Madelia while trying to avoid arrest. That man's wife was killed by a train just before the man was killed." Shaking his head, the lieutenant added, "It's all pretty confusing at this point."

"Please, I need to be alone," Lacy said, standing.

"I'm not sure it's a good idea for you to be alone," the lieutenant said, also getting to his feet. "Is there someone we can call to come and stay with you? I'll be happy to take you anywhere you want to go."

"No, thank you," Lacy said, forcing a smile. "I'll be alright. Thank you for coming by."

Shaking his head, the lieutenant turned and left—a decision he would regret for the rest of his life. Lacy McMurphy was the only person on the planet who had a total picture—or at least as clear a picture as such a tangled web of events would ever offer.

Alone in the living room, Lacy collapsed into an overstuffed chair and sat for a long time staring off into space, too stunned to cry. She would never see her beloved husband again, never kiss his lips, hear his laughter, feel the warmth of his embrace. Martin McMurphy had dared stand for something and had paid for it with his life.

Only then did she realize that she hadn't asked Lieutenant Statements where they had taken Martin. It was a call she'd have to make, but not at that moment. At that moment, it was time to cry—to open up her soul and cry as she never cried before.

As the sobs tore at her heart, Lacy wondered what that superintendent had to do with Martin—to the point where her husband would kill him. She could understand why Chimlyn Johnson would have killed Badge, but why would Junior Beane follow Martin to the site of a suicide and kill him?

After an hour of fruitless soul-searching, Lacy got up and walked slowly into the kitchen, where she poured herself a glass of Franzia, a wine both she and Martin had always loved. Then she went back out to the living room and sat in the same chair, her mind a spinning mass of confusion.

Badge's wife had killed herself after involving Martin. Badge had been killed by a bird after being kidnapped by a disturbed man—who was then killed by a policeman while trying to avoid arrest shortly after the man's wife had been killed in a collision with a train. As far as Lacy was concerned, all three of those people, and Agnes Pullet, for that matter, had been killed because of Badge Pullet. Now Martin had been added to that list—but was there anything she could have done to put an end to that terrible chain of events?

Suddenly her pondering was interrupted by the front doorbell. What could it be now?

"Trick or treat!" said two happy youngsters standing on her porch, holding their bags out in front of them while their mother waited on the sidewalk in front of the house.

Numbly, Lacy reached into a bowl beside the door and dropped two Snickers bars into each child's bag. She smiled as best she could as they said thank you and turned to go. Her world had ground to a halt, yet other people were still living and laughing.

Then she shut off the porch light to let all treat-or-treaters know she wouldn't be handing out any more candy that night. She needed to be alone, and she just couldn't face all those happy children—children she would have relished interacting with on any other Halloween night.

Just to be safe, she turned out all the lights in the living room and went upstairs to the bedroom, carrying her wine glass in her trembling hand. She flopped down on the bed and stared at the streetlights shining in the darkness. She could hear the muffled sounds of laughter from the street as children went from house to house.

Where was solace to be found? Where had God been when all that evil was being spread for so long? Where was God now, when she needed consolation more than ever? Why did good people stand by and let mean, ugly things continue to happen? Lacy's thoughts raced unchecked through her mind and she was overwhelmed by the flood of emotions she could neither control nor understand.

Finally, her tears would no longer come, but the thoughts raged as strongly as ever. How could one human being be the cause of so much pain, suffering, and death? How could all the goodness that she and Martin had believed in have been washed away so completely?

Her mind began to repeat a mantra that at first made no sense. "Is this all there is? Just this? Just this? Just this? JusThis?"

She had arrived at a point of loneliness from which there was no escape, yet she longed to fly far away from all the dark intentions born of mankind.

She didn't realize how it had happened, but some time later, she felt the cold steel of the shotgun barrel as she slipped it into her mouth. It had a bitter metallic taste, but it wasn't unpleasant. In the darkness of her despair, her brightly-painted big toe found its way to the trigger. It was cool to the touch, but again not unpleasant.

Disturbed only momentarily by the report of a shotgun blast, the pigeons roosting in the parking ramp continued to coo softly, as only pigeons or doves could do.

—Epilogue—

We all struggle against the torrential waves of the unscrupulous, clinging to the shifting shores of trust only to be pulled into the chilly depths by deceitful intentions. Evil maintains, evil gains, and evil destroys. Humans will forever be haunted by the unjustness of things and the agonizing presence of the self-absorbed and the evil, bloated, noxious ego.

An accomplished liar in a position of trust can wreak havoc on the lives of untold numbers of innocent people. They use their control to manipulate minds and hearts, spreading untruth and bending the will of the people to match their own twisted designs. Innocent mistakes are fodder for dishonest lust. Mistakes provide the mechanism of control for manipulative minds. Those minds then ejaculate untruths and grunt in putrid satisfaction over their ill-gotten gains.

We all want to put our best foot forward and to be persons of distinction, but we're forever being pulled into the shadows by the unscrupulous. Try as we may, we can't avoid the shadows. The creatures of deceit will never let us walk forever in the sunshine. They will always hide behind the façade of justice to make us do their deceitful bidding. We can never truly be free from their evil clutches.

When the dust had settled in Normal and the surrounding area, six people were dead, and no one was ever able to make any real sense of it. Jakes Stadium pizza parlor in Normal continued to be busy and the talk around town was that it was unusual for Normal to be on CNN or the AP.

As everyone understood it, a woman was following her husband and got hit by a train. Her husband was chased and shot by cops in Madelia. The cops found the Normal police chief's badge in the husband's pocket. They found the chief's car abandoned in a Normal cemetery. The chief's buried body was discovered. There were several antique glass pictures of the state capital found in the trunk of the chief's car. Phone records showed that the husband from Madelia had called Martin McMurphy, who had been dismissed from the Normal police force due to charges of drug activity.

Meanwhile, Normal's mayor had taken full advantage of the national exposure, going on the various new media to tell the world that Charles Pullet had been the best police chief the town had ever known. The governor attended his funeral and the press had a field day, calling Charles Pullet a true American hero. Townspeople were shown on television crying at his loss and saying how much everyone loved him.

Sitting in the pizza parlor one Friday afternoon, Mr. Jankowski, normally considered the town's resident crazy old coot, was no exception. He summed up his theory as to what had happened to a news reporter.

"That son of a bitch, Martin McMurphy, was on dope and had the chief killed, I'm tellin' ya. Badge Pullet was a damn good cop and a real sharp dresser. You never saw a single strand of hair out of place on his head. The whole town's gonna miss him, I tell ya. Then McMurphy came along and killed him. That's why his wife blew her own head off. She couldn't live with the fact that she'd married such a loser. I heard 'bout them rumors that the chief was up to no good on his office computer, but the mayor cleared that up. Damn right! He said nothin' happened!"

As the reporter dutifully took notes, Jankowski added, "Then the chief's wife went out and killed herself because she couldn't stand losing such a fine husband. I'll bet that McMurphy killed the chief or had one of his druggie buddies do it. Then Junior Beane stuck a knife in him before the truth could come out. I think McMurphy had it coming. After all, Junior figured that McMurphy was messing with his wife. Junior did us all a favor by doin' away with the bastard. It woulda cost the taxpayers plenty, believe you me, to put him away. Like lots of other folks around here, I'm gonna send the Beanes some cold hard cash to help Junior get off."

When the reporter talked to other patrons in the restaurant, they generally agreed with Jankowski's assessment of the chain of events that had put Normal in the spotlight nationwide.

Corruption is and always has been imbedded into the fabric of governmental systems. When a simple truth is revealed that might be construed as threatening, action is quickly taken to silence the voice of truth. The status quo must be maintained. Words are used to confuse and impede. The reins of power are held tightly in the hands of a few privileged individuals.

As the old saying goes, power corrupts and absolute power corrupts absolutely. We are required to confront our daily decisions with pride and determination, and we must see our mistakes as life's opportunities for learning. It is ignorance that binds evil to goodness.

JUSTHIS

When we hold others accountable for committing the wrongful acts, then do those same things ourselves, we are hypocrites. It is, as it always shall be.

> Vintery, mintery, cutery, corn,
> Apple seed and apple thorn.
> Wire, briar, limber lock,
> Three geese in a flock.
> One flew east,
> One flew west,
> And one flew over the cuckoo's nest.